One Part Human
An Obscure Magic Book 1

By

Viola Grace

Benny has lived her life in the shadows, avoiding the public eye. Her life as a recipe blogger pays the bills and lets her socialise, but she is about to get the assignment of a lifetime.

Her boss orders her into a one-week ride-along with agents of the XIA, the eXtranormal Investigation Agency. It is the anniversary of the agency, and they need to improve their exposure with the general public.

Against her objections, she is paired with a standard set of agents—a vampire, a shifter and a fey. They are willing to work with her, and it is only when she signs the waivers that she learns why. They all read her column.

A week doesn't seem like much time to learn about an organisation that deals with things most folk don't enjoy thinking about, but it whips past when the assignments go from casual crime to murders that have one pivot point. Benny.

Chapter One

$\mathcal{B}$enny hated assignment meetings. They were intolerable, as those selected for the lackluster jobs tried to squirm out of them. Today was no exception.

"I don't see why I am up for this particular assignment, Julian. Doing a week of ride-alongs with the XIA is not my idea of scintillating reporting. What am I going to do? Get stuck in a black van for a week?"

The gathered reporters were all staring at her with amusement and relief that it wasn't them.

"Benny, you have basic magic senses and two years of mage studies at the university. You are the most capable of seeing if the XIA is actually worth the money we have put in over the last fifty years or if the anniversary is celebrating mediocrity." Julian rubbed his green-scaled hands together. "Add to that the fact that you are human and it makes you the perfect foil to the extranatural officers that you will be dealing with."

Benny scrubbed her hands through her hair. "This isn't a good idea. I just want to write the recipe articles and information on how to carve pumpkins for the best light distribution at Halloween."

Julian drummed his nails on the table, and he let out a gust of air. "Do you want me to spell this out?"

"Please."

He waved at the selection of reporters in the room and on displays. "None of us can pass for human, and therefore, the XIA would consider us a suspect if they forgot we were there for the article."

Benny covered her eyes with one hand for a moment before glaring at the occupants of the room. "They don't do that."

Freddy was next to her, and she nodded. "They do think we are up to no good."

Benny gave her friend a sideways look. "In your case, they are right."

Freddy shrugged. "I have to be me."

"Freddy, it is when you take someone else's identification that you have a problem." Julian sighed. "Right. Settled. Benny, you are on the XIA, and they are expecting you for the nightshift. Go home, get some sleep and take notes on everything you can. They aren't allowing photos, but that is to be expected. I trust your memory and your common sense. Everyone else. As we have stated, get to it."

He pushed himself to his feet and walked over to Benny, she turned so he was staring at her face. "Take care and don't do anything that Freddy would do."

From behind her, Benny heard, "Hey!"

"For a full week?"

"It is the fiftieth year of the XIA. It needs a full week of examination, and we are the only news agency they are willing to deal with. More to the point, you are the only reporter they are willing to deal with. Apparently, they like food."

Benny nodded, grabbed her notepad and her tablet and got to her feet, topping the goblin by close to two feet. He didn't have a problem being even with her boobs, and she didn't even notice it after a few years.

Freddy linked arms with her and asked, "So, did you want to start happy hour a little early?"

"No. I have to run this past Mom and Dad. You know how they feel about the XIA."

Freddy let out a gusty sigh. "Did you want me to come with you?"

"Nope, but thanks for the offer. I will keep you posted on anything interesting that you can investigate for the gossip column."

"Appreciate it, Benny. Have a good night and don't forget to write down anything interesting about the officers you are with." Freddy wagged her eyebrows suggestively, and Benny sighed.

"I will consider it if there is anything noteworthy. I have never actually been in the XIA offices before."

"Few humans have."

Benny snickered and headed to her desk, leaving Freddy flirting with the copy guy.

She stuffed everything she needed into her bag and headed for the door. It was just past eleven, so her parents should be getting ready for lunch.

She called her father and warned him that she was on her way.

"Do you want some lunch?"

Benny smiled evilly, "Only if it is no trouble."

"No trouble. See you in half an hour."

"Love you, Dad."

"Love you, Benny."

She hung up and did a little dance. Her mother's lunches were nothing to be sneered at.

Benny's stomach was groaning happily as she finished her third course. Soup, salad and half a roast chicken had gone to the next life via her plate.

"You had better have room for dessert, Beneficia." Her mother was smiling as she made the warning.

"I will be able to manage something." She grinned, and her father grinned back while her mother went to get coffee. Her mom stared at her across the expanse of the counter. "Now, why are you here today, darling?"

"Now, before I say anything that will upset you, know that I am not pregnant, this isn't about a boy and I am not being arrested."

Her father sat back and drummed his fingers on the table. "I would be in favour of all but the last. You need to meet someone, pet."

"I know, Dad."

She cleared her throat and took the coffee her mother handed to her. "I will be spending a week in a ride-along with the XIA. I can't get out of it and still keep my job."

Both of her parents turned to stone in that moment. Two heads turned to look at her with horror in their gazes.

"You know how dangerous that will be for you, Benny." Her father took her hand.

She gripped his calloused fingers. "I know. But it should be fine. I am just writing about their protocols and the division of departments."

Her mother put a strawberry shortcake in front of her. "The eXtranormal Intervention Agency is not safe for you, darling."

"I know, Mom, but I won't be spending a lot of time in the office. I will be with them in a vehicle."

Her dad leaned forward. "And if the shifter can smell your blood?"

Her mom scowled. "Or the fey or the vampire."

"Then, they smell that I have a complicated family tree. I figured that out when I was six."

It had been a school project that her father had lit on fire, and he had spoken with her teacher, and the woman had allowed little Benny to paint a portrait of her mother instead.

Benny continued. "Lots of people have mixed family trees nowadays."

Her mother shook her head. "Not like you, pet." Her mom came over and stroked her hair.

Benny hugged her with one arm and let her mom stroke her hair a little more. She shared a look with her father, happy to be in her mother's arms and he smiled briefly, the memory of their near brush with sadness flickering in his eyes. It had been fifteen years, and they still felt the panic of those first weeks of her mom's diagnosis any time she touched them. Cancer sucked.

Smiling brightly, Benny sat up straight and attacked her dessert. "I will be fine. I will make some concealer and get through the next week with all the grace and style you two gave me."

Her father nodded. "Good thinking. Better safe than sorry. I will help you."

They all sat around and finished dessert. Her father did the dishes, and when all was tidy, they headed to the herb garden for the ingredients they needed to craft a draught that would keep Benny's blend of ancestors from rising and being noticed.

It was just another kind of cooking, and Benny had gained her passion for it honestly.

The taste of strawberry kept coming up as Benny walked up the steps of the XIA. At the door, she showed her credentials and let her bag be searched. The scanner was what she was worried about.

She went through the glyph-covered archway, and it glowed softly. The officer monitoring it smacked the side of the terminal he was looking at and smiled. "Go on in, Miss Ganger, it is always going off."

She was given her visitor's pass and sent past the final checkpoint into the offices of the XIA by an officer with the focussed stare of a shifter.

She nodded and followed his quick direction to the briefing room where her agents were waiting to meet her.

The plaques on the wall gave her clear direction through the maze, and she could see the magical glyphs on all doorways and at even spacing throughout the hall. This place was protected against violence and demonic interference from the ground to the highest level. There were no shenanigans of an extranatural nature here.

When she got to the briefing room, she knocked and waited until she heard the call to come in.

She wished she was nervous. She should be nervous, but nervous never came to her easily. Curiosity was her motivating emotional factor.

She identified the lawyer first, the captain second and the three agents that she would be riding with were lined up and visually taking her in.

"Miss Ganger. Welcome. I am Captain Matheson. This is the primary counsel for the XIA, Ms. Wingart. She has a release form for you to sign as well as additional waivers that you need to go over."

"Of course."

The winged fey Captain smiled at her. "Please, have a seat. The sooner we can get you signed in, the sooner we can release the men for their rounds. And yourself of course."

"Oh, of course."

A few of the glyphs on the wall glowed, and Benny realised that the lawyer was trying to glamour her.

She settled down and looked over the first page quickly. "You can keep the glamour. I am trying to get this over with as much as you are. Making your skin shiny and your boobs perky isn't really something I care about."

She heard the lawyer gasp, and she signed the first document after striking out the segment that indicated her family would not be alerted to the reasons for her injury.

She flipped on to the second and third forms and signed away her right to photograph the details. She crossed out the inability to report on anything that she had seen, writing in that she would respect the privacy of the officers and those witnessed through the ride-along. No proper names or addresses would be used.

She signed off on it with those changes and slid it back to the five-foot pixie.

The woman flicked her a look through heavily made-up lashes. "You have some magical training."

"Just enough to keep me from doing anything stupid."

"These terms are acceptable." The fey put her own signature to them, and the captain followed suit.

The counsellor picked up her paper-work and headed out of the room. The moment she cleared it, the three agents applauded.

The captain shook his head. "Knock it off, guys. Miss Ganger, these are the agents you will be riding with. Agent Treble, Smith and Argyle. This is Miss Ganger of the Redbird City News."

Agent Treble was the elf, and he inclined his head. "You are the one with the delightful cooking articles."

"Apparently."

Agent Smith was the shifter. He had lovely golden eyes that smiled when he said, "They really are good."

Agent Argyle had deep red hair and chalk-white skin. He was some sort of undead, or she would eat her laptop.

"I don't know about food, but I will trust their judgement. It isn't that they jerk off to your articles, but they come pretty close."

"Argyle!" The captain rolled his eyes.

The undead showed his fangs as he grinned. "Apologies, sir."

"Be polite; Miss Ganger has agreed to the ride-along under duress. It is the XIA's fiftieth anniversary, and we need to make a good impression. Be on your best behaviour."

They snapped to their feet and saluted sharply.

Benny blinked and backed up in her chair when they moved. She had seen images of the XIA. Height was a factor.

If they could intimidate a perpetrator, they were ahead of the game. You couldn't be weak and take down a shifter or a fey or one of the undead. They were all in good physical form, and she had to stop herself from staring.

They seemed to get taller as she stared, but that was only because they approached and each shook her hand.

"Pleased to meet you, Miss Ganger," was said by each one.

Somehow, she got to her feet and looked at them one by one. "So, when do we get going?"

Agent Smith grinned. "That would be now."

$\mathcal{B}$enny sat in the back with Agent Tremble. She was strapped in while he and the others were not. It was part of her contract.

"So, Miss Ganger, where did you get the recipe for mini-mushroom quiches?" Agent Smith asked her from the front passenger seat. Argyle was driving.

"My mother is an excellent cook, and she and my father used to entertain frequently. She hosted a number of different species at the dinner parties, and I would help her."

"Used to?" Agent Tremble raised his eyebrows, the pale, graceful lines rising toward the platinum blond of his hair.

His hair, as well as that of the other two, was fastened tightly at the base of his neck with only two long tendrils falling to either side of his very elegant features.

"Yes, my mother was ill several years ago, and since then, my family has drawn in on itself. She helps me work out the recipes and change things to keep them modern and doable for today's cooks."

"Well, if my mother cooked half as good as you did, I never would have left home." Agent Smith grinned. "I wouldn't have been able to; I would weigh nine hundred pounds."

"His pride would have eaten him." Agent Tremble laughed.

Well, that settled it. She was with an elf, a vampire and a lion. Her chance of surviving the night was pretty good.

A call came in, and Smith took it. He keyed in the address and Argyle turned their SUV and they spun off into the night.

The shift she was on began at eight and ended at four in the morning. It was eight thirty right now. Seven and a half hours of holding on for dear life as they whipped through the night. At least they weren't on horseback.

Argyle grinned at her in the mirror. "We don't have a siren; she is on desk duty."

Benny smiled and giggled.

Tremble chuckled. "It is an old joke, but we like it."

Smith turned his head. "We are heading to a fey-fey altercation. We won't ask you to stay in the car, but don't stray too far from it. You are here to see us operate, but we don't want you in danger, Miss Ganger."

"Call me Benny."

Tremble looked over at her with surprise. "Benny?"

"Yes." She didn't tell him what it was short for. Beneficia was not a common first name. Benny was socially acceptable just about anywhere.

"That wasn't the name we were given when we were first briefed."

She wrinkled her nose. "Probably not, but it is the one that I will answer to."

"Fair enough."

Their vehicle was travelling at high speed through an exceptionally wealthy neighbourhood. They approached a gate, and Argyle flipped a switch. The gates swung open and let them through.

Benny could hear screaming and see flares of fey magic from where she was sitting. She leaned back as Argyle brought the vehicle to a sudden halt. The other three were out their doors and heading for the altercation without a word.

She unbuckled her seatbelt and slipped out of the SUV. It wasn't hard to follow the others. The shrieking fight between the fey was impossible to miss.

Benny was surprised by the two clumps of dazed humans, seven in all. Tremble grabbed the male fey, Argyle grabbed the female and Smith called for a pickup van and medical assistance.

Tremble spoke calmly as he forced his prisoner to his knees. The female suffered the same fate from Argyle.

"Now, what is the cause of all this?"

The man snarled, "It was my day with the pool and hot tub. She had it last night."

The female with deep-blue hair that seemed quite natural, based on the colour of her pubic hair glowing through the gauzy gown she was wearing, hissed. "It is still my turn. They are the same lovers."

Argyle closed his eyes slowly, and he was obviously counting to ten. "Smith, did you call for medical?"

"I did."

"Have them bring some iron supplements. Those humans need restoration and protection. They are fey locked."

Benny stared with her eyes wide. The male fey looked over at her and said, "Hello, beautiful. When this lot is hauled off, would you care to stay and play?"

His erection tented his loose trousers, and she felt the pull of his glamour.

His wife caught on and smiled slyly at her. "Yes, lovely. Stay and play."

The amount of magic being used on her was obscene, as were the images they were casting at her. She blinked and smiled weakly. "You know, that sounds like so much fun."

She steeled her voice. "Except that parasites like you two make me sick, and preying on deliberately chosen, powerless humans throws you right into that category, making you subject to the magical abduction, assault and confinement charges. Seven counts by my guess, because even if they wanted it, they couldn't legally want it."

She flicked their power back at them, and both of them were out cold in an instant.

The humans collapsed a moment later.

Smith looked at her in surprise with a grin on his lips. "Can we keep you?"

She blushed and stood back while they cuffed the fey and carried the humans to the front of the expansive home.

Tremble came to her side as their backup took away the two fey in the prisoner transport. "We aren't all like that."

She patted his arm. "I know you aren't. This isn't the first round of fey I have met. My parents used to socialise, remember?"

"Ah. You do seem very resistant to mental seduction."

She grinned. "They should have bought me nachos and a hotdog. I roll over for that."

Smith passed her and made a quick note, muttering, "Nachos and a hot dog."

She blushed again, but got back in the vehicle while they completed checking on the humans and making sure that there were none left in the house. Smith did the check.

Benny sat down and made notes about the evening so far.

When the medical attendants arrived, there were three ambulances, and they divided the victims relatively evenly, putting IVs in several and urging them into the vehicles. They were on their way in six minutes.

Her privacy disappeared in the next moment, because the guys climbed into the car, and they were off again.

She sat for three minutes before asking. "So, what do you guys think of the use of the term extranatural instead of supernatural?"

Argyle shrugged. "It is more appropriate. We are more than we were."

Tremble laughed, "And the fey don't care. Extranatural, extranormal. We are both."

"Extra-ego." Smith smirked.

Argyle looked at her in the rear-view. "You have a little extranatural in your nature, don't you, Benny?"

She shrugged. "I suppose, but since the great wave two hundred years ago, we all have bits of magical creatures in us, even if we don't know it."

Tremble smiled, "If you had a magical creature in you, you would know it."

It took her two seconds to blush.

Smith shot back, "Not if it was you. She would need an enlargement enchantment and a magnifying glass."

Argyle ducked and focused on the driving as Smith and Tremble had a slap fight. A second call broke it up, and Smith had to take it.

It was amazing to see them shut down and resume their business as agents. They went from teen boys to adults in under a second.

She stared out the window as they swung from the elegant neighbourhood to one far more middle class.

Smith turned, "We have been called out for a disorderly werewolf. I suspect first shift, but I won't know until I meet him."

Tremble snorted. "We are doing backup."

"Where should I be?"

Smith sighed, "For this one, remain in the vehicle. We don't know where he is or how his thoughts are processing at the moment."

Argyle was sombre. "I will lock the doors."

It was as much of a warning as they could give her. She knew what happened to those who ran afoul of newly shifted weres. They usually ended up in the emergency room with permanent scarring, if someone got to them fast enough.

She sat in the vehicle with the lights off, making notes. The agents went to the home that the call had emanated from, and Smith and Argyle began tracking the shifter.

Benny really wanted to be out there with them, because inside the vehicle, she felt like a staked goat.

Smith shifted his head, and his lion's mane was glaringly obvious even in the darkness. He took off down an alleyway toward a back lane, and Argyle followed while Tremble stayed on alert.

Benny froze when a shadow moved close to the vehicle. She heard the light scratching of claws on asphalt and the ticking as it paced closer. Benny had been around enough shifters to know when one was hunting.

She unclasped the seatbelt as quietly as she could and eased it away from her, holding it so it didn't make a sound as it rested in place. She shifted herself to the centre of the vehicle while he wasn't looking, but every time she moved, he lifted his head.

Tremble hadn't caught on to his proximity. He was on the wrong side of the vehicle for his patchy and fluffy body to be visible to the elf.

He sniffed along the doorframe next to her original seat. She was fascinating to some species; it came from her blended family tree. According to her grandmother, many species wanted to get in on that kind of power. They would do what it took to be part of the next generation.

She watched his half-shifted back hunch down, and then, his head snapped up, his jaws parted and his gleaming tongue came out. The orange of his eyes was hot with a combination of lust and fury. Yup, he was a teenager.

Benny tried not to flinch as he flicked at the handle of the door, trying to get it to open. He would only work with his human instincts for so long, and then, he was coming through that door.

She whispered a repelling charm and one to reinforce the door.

He blinked and stumbled back as the first charm struck him.

The roar in the darkness was a relief. There was nothing like the bellow of a lion to make a young dog cower.

The young man submitted immediately. Smith cuffed him and hauled him off down the street.

Argyle and Tremble met with the initial caller and then returned to the SUV.

Tremble grinned, and she scooted away from his seat and back to her spot behind the driver.

"It was your little charm that got my attention. You repelled him very well."

Benny smiled weakly. "He was trying to get into the car, so it seemed the best course of action."

Tremble put his hand on her shoulder, and Argyle hissed, "No contact, Tremble. Those are the rules."

"She's upset, Argyle."

"Rules are rules, and we are on duty."

Tremble pulled his hand away with a sigh. "Sorry. Our job does take us to places where a lone female is endangered."

"Only because most races refuse to teach their females to hunt and kill for fear of the men being thought obsolete."

She buckled up, and they drove the SUV to follow Smith to the house where the young lad had made his escape from. His family was in the yard, and lights streamed out. Smith brought him home as they pulled up, and the youngling was alternately hugged and struck in the head with the back of a hand by other shifters.

When Smith had finished admonishing the family on how to get their son into therapy for his change, he returned to their vehicle and resumed his human visage.

"Well, done, Benny. You kept calm and let him remain next to your window until he tried to get in. That was enough time for me to come around. After this is over, I am going to file a request to get you assigned to us."

The other guys laughed, and they were called to their next mission. There was an undead committing petty crimes, and they were now free to chase it down. Argyle was going to have to take point on this one.

Chapter Three

Three petty extranormal robberies, followed by a hooker with no actual genitalia and two disgruntled customers.

Benny had never seen a mer-woman as a hooker before, but she made a convincing argument for never intending to furnish the half-elves with sexual services. She was trading her magic and the touch of her mouth.

They locked her up for unlawful spell peddling. Magic—you could give it away, but if you wanted to charge for it, you needed a license.

"Why do you turn your prisoners over to the other agents?"

The hooker was on her way to booking. Smith entered the details of the arrest into the computer in the SUV, and he grimaced. "We separate it to speed the process along. As agents, it is our job to investigate, not to continue the interrogation. The prisoners will be interrogated at the office and processed according to what they have been charged with."

Tremble smiled. "Argyle and Smith are the best agents to do the data entry. I am not comfortable with technology."

Smith muttered, "He means he can't type."

Argyle snickered as they rolled out again, "Or spell."

Tremble flipped them off and turned to her, "So, Benny, are you finding this ride-along educational?"

"So far, it is very interesting. I had no idea of the range of the calls you were sent out on."

Tremble laughed. "You haven't seen anything. We also do speeches for the Changeling Guides and Scouts, the newly undead and the Fey Integration Association. We go out, speak and then get back to work."

"What about the Mage Guides and Scouts?"

"They are on their own. Human officers deal with them."

She nodded. "Right."

She had never fit in in the Mage Guides, but it had been the only option for her. She didn't appear to be anything other than human, but the magic was in her blood. Her sash still hung proudly on the wall of her parents' study.

Smith looked up from his keyboard, "Were you in the Guides?"

She blinked. "Uh, yeah."

Tremble smiled and a wicked gleam came to his eyes. "I bet you looked adorable in that uniform."

She gave him a bland look. "From time to time I still do."

Argyle's shoulders shook as he chortled.

Tremble sighed and smiled blissfully. "Well, my dreams are set for the next week."

Benny grinned, and she settled into her place as pervert mascot to this gathering of officers.

"So, when do we eat?"

Smith smiled. "Thank goodness. Someone else with an appetite...for food. Argyle, tacos!"

Argyle muttered about basic human necessities, and he pulled a U-turn, heading for Benny's part of town.

Taco! Taco! Taco! was her favourite haunt when she went out with Freddy, but she had never been there in the wee hours. It was after midnight and not yet dawn, so she was on new territory with a bunch of XIA agents.

Dem-rah was the chef on duty, and he waved at Benny cheerfully, all four arms waving. "Benny, darling. What can I get for you?"

"Three chicken, two beef and plenty of hot sauce." She looked over and nodded. "And a coke."

He got her order, took her money and turned to her companions with a cold face. "Agents, what can I get for you?"

Smith and Tremble ordered, their food was served, but it didn't look anything like Benny's.

Argyle sat at a picnic table and sipped at a thermos. Apparently, he brought his own.

She looked at Dem-rah as she wrestled for a straw. "While the agents seem willing to eat anything, please give them the same calibre of food that you serve to me and my friends."

"They are with you?" He raised his brows and snatched the food back before the agents could grab it. Smith looked like he wanted to cry.

"I am doing a ride-along for the article. One week for the XIA anniversary." She smiled. "It is really very interesting so far."

She munched one of the tacos and groaned happily. "I might have to start waking Freddy up before dawn and hauling her over here. It is worth it."

Dem-rah beamed. "Gratitude for the compliment. It means much coming from you."

She winked and joined Argyle at the table. She worked her way through her delightfully spicy tacos in soft shells and sighed happily when she was done.

Smith looked at the food suspiciously, but Tremble dove in. He moaned and sauce covered his pearly skin. Smith took the hint, and he was halfway through his platter of ten when he picked the mass up and went back to order another ten tacos.

When he came back, he smiled at his new treasures. "When this is over, do you mind if I wake you up in the middle of the night to act as my food liaison?"

She laughed. "Probably. Dem-rah is an excellent cook, but his brother had two arms broken by overzealous XIA agents twenty years ago and spider goblins hold a grudge. You were getting the health-code special. It met all the codes...barely."

Smith sighed. "It still tasted damned good."

Tremble daintily cleaned his face with a napkin. His lips were slightly swollen from the chili sauce, but he looked happy.

Smith destroyed the second set of ten, and Argyle looked at them wistfully. "I never ate a taco."

Benny acted on reflex, and she extended her arm. "Here you go. It is still active in the bloodstream."

He blinked. "Are you sure?"

"Just a taste. I am sure the others would help pry you off if necessary."

"They might have to."

"I heal quickly so I digest quickly. If you want to taste taco, you had better bite now."

He flashed his teeth and bit her wrist. She focussed on providing him with the taste of dinner and downplaying what was all in her bloodstream.

She counted to five before she tapped his cheek. After that, she clenched her fist and put pressure on her vein to remove the flow.

He lifted his head drowsily. "So, that is a taco. There was a lot more going on in there than human magic, but thank you. Few folk realise that a little donation does not bind them to a vamp."

"I had a decent education. My parents raised me right."

She pressed the puncture wounds and tried to get them to stop.

Smith sighed and took her forearm, licking his tongue across the wounds. They sealed up, and she was soon back to fighting form.

"Thank you." She smiled.

Argyle was looking at her with a sober expression. "Thank you. It was an honour to have tasted you."

"I would have to second Argyle's statement. I could get drunk on the taste of your skin, Benny."

"Not an option. We are on business. I was just upset that Argyle had not experienced Dem-rah's tacos."

Argyle looked at her with assessment in his gaze. "You are not afraid of any of us, are you?"

She shrugged. "Nope. I have met people from most species and guilds over my life. My parents used to entertain a lot."

"Politicians?" Tremble arched his brows.

She shook her head. "No. Academics."

He chuckled. "That would explain it. You have a self-contained manner that I usually associate with humans in their fifth or sixth decade."

She smiled and inclined her head. "I will take that as a compliment."

"You should. A woman who cannot appreciate the past holds little appeal for most men with family histories."

Argyle chuckled and licked his lips again, "Or personal ones."

Tremble chuckled. "That, too."

Benny clutched her hands to her chest and said on a breathy gasp. "So I might be good enough for a man one day? Oh, joy! I never thought such a thing would be possible. Butt-heads."

Smith's shoulders were shaking as he covered his mouth with one hand. Finally, he said, "Keep your compliments, Tremble. The lady neither needs nor wants your approval."

Benny waggled her eyebrows as she finished her soda. With a last slurp, she tossed the cup to the garbage can. A hand shot out and pulled the trash inside.

Tremble blinked his pretty eyes.

Smith chuckled. "Trash troll?"

"Yup. One of the best recyclers in the last ten years. That can probably weigh around four hundred pounds."

Argyle turned his head to look over the street. "Anything else lurking around that we should know about?"

"Nothing out of the ordinary. Same old, same old." She got to her feet and headed over to Dem-rah. "Any chance that I can get your spice mix recipe out of you tonight?"

"Ah, Benny, only if you were my wife. So, I am afraid that it will not happen. Your father would kill me if I tried." He winked.

"Yes, in an extremely unpleasant manner. Ah well, it was worth asking."

He winked and got back to cleaning. "It is always worth asking."

She returned to the XIA agents with a series of hand wipes, and she distributed them with a smile. "What happens next?"

Smith straightened, "We get back in our vehicle and wait for the next call."

They got to their feet and headed for their transport. Benny followed along and settled into her spot, buckling the seatbelt and waiting.

Argyle drove down the street at a normal speed, and when a call came through, they were off.

Chapter Four

A pugnacious zombie was refusing to accept last call, so Argyle took their group to The Hyde.

Benny had been to the nightclub twice in her life, and neither time was particularly memorable. This one definitely made it one for the books.

Tremble ordered her to stay in the car. "Lock the doors. This time of the morning, most things out here are hungry."

She nodded and stayed in the dark of the SUV.

The XIA agents went into the club, and it was six silent minutes before the doors burst open and Smith tumbled out with what she hoped was their target.

The lion shifter was beating the undead into the pavement, and Argyle and Tremble came out after them.

She saw Tremble calling in a pickup, and then, she turned her attention back to the zombie giving as good as he was getting.

There was snarling and gnashing of teeth on both parts. Two minutes later, the hauler arrived, and Tremble stepped forward, wrapping the zombie in bands of fey magic. Argyle stepped in and loaded the zombie into the storage case that had been brought out for him. He would remain boxed up until he calmed down. That would probably be sometime after Friday night. Zombies were notoriously vulnerable to alcohol and caffeine.

Argyle held him in the case while Tremble locked him down. To Benny's surprise, they were wearing black gloves that they stripped off and dumped in the biohazard container inside the transport vehicle. Even Smith was wearing the gloves, and he peeled them off, tossing them with distaste.

The drivers of the pickup vehicle handed Smith some wipes, and he rubbed every part of himself with them to remove the zombie smell.

Benny hid her smirk as they joined her again. At least they got to get physical on their shift. She had the feeling that she was holding them back a bit.

It was the last bit of excitement on her first night.

Two more hours of hashing the events of the evening for her article and she was ready to go home. They pulled into the XIA lot, and the moment they were parked, she hopped out of their vehicle.

After the zombie fight, the air had been a little thick in the SUV, so breathing fresh air became a luxury.

She stepped away from the vehicle and made sure she had her notes and her purse.

Tremble leaned against their SUV. "So, Miss Benny, same time tomorrow?"

She chuckled. "You mean later today? Yes. I will be here. Four more shifts with you guys before the anniversary. I have more research to do."

Smith looked at her with concern. "Are you all right to drive home?"

"Aw, how sweet. Yes, of course I am. All I have done tonight is hang out in the car."

Argyle inclined his head. "It was an entertaining first evening."

She bowed to them all. "Thank you for improving my education."

With her shoulders back, she headed to her car, starting it up with a flick of her keychain.

She opened the door and chucked her purse into the passenger seat. She slid behind the wheel, and the car roared with excitement before she even put the key in.

"Down boy. We are going." She stroked her dashboard and checked the mirrors. Everything was clear, so she got underway to get herself home.

Driving an enchanted car was not for everyone, but Benny was confident enough in the car to take it anywhere and let it take over if it needed to. She called it Pooky, but it used to be a Pukha.

The earliest touches of dawn were sparking, threatening to bloom. Benny drove back to her home and sighed happily when she parked next to the dower house.

She dragged herself and her stuff into the house. "Morning, Jessamine."

The house's ghost smiled and whispered. "How did it go?"

"I need a shower and sleep. The agents were fine."

"Just fine? That isn't the chatter in the spectrum. I have heard that the agent teams are fine physical specimens."

"They are, and I will talk to you about them when I wake up."

"Fair enough. Your room is ready."

Benny removed her jacket and hung it up. Her shoes went flying, and she peeled off her clothing on the way to her shower. Jessamine was her housekeeper and companion, and she liked the cleaning. Benny was in no mood to stop her.

Half an hour later, she was wrapped in a towel with another on her head, flipping through her notes and transcribing them onto her computer in a rough outline.

Jessamine blacked out the coming dawn and edged the computer away from her until Benny caught the hint. "Good night, Jess."

"Good morning, Benny. Have a nice rest."

The room was dim and quiet. Benny leaned back and pulled the sheets over her, trying to rest before she had to go back.

The moment she closed her eyes, images of her agents danced through her mind. Their dancing eventually slowed, and her mind slowed enough to sleep.

Benny glared at the sunset and checked her phone. "Jess, did you change my wallpaper again?"

Jessamine floated over. "No. Why do you ask?"

Benny turned it to face her. "Because I have never seen a picture of a kitten in a sailor suit on my phone before now."

"Maybe he just crawled in there." Jessamine smiled.

"I doubt it. It isn't Fleet Week. No sailors should be creeping around in my phone." She tapped the back of her phone with her finger. "Put the starscape back."

"I don't have time. Your parents would like to see you at the big house."

"When?"

"As soon as you woke up?" Jessamine wrinkled her nose. "Sorry. I forgot."

"Damn, damn, damn." She raced to her room and put on her clothing for the evening of sitting in a car.

The black button-down shirt would hide any stains if anything happened to smack into her. She didn't know if they were hitting Dem-rah's joint again, but she was willing to take that chance.

Her bag, phone, wallet and notebook were with her as she got into her car and blazed a path the two kilometres to her parents' very large abode.

Gravel flew as she braked and threw her car into park. She grabbed her bag and headed into the place she had grown up.

Her mother greeted her in the hallway. "Oh, sweetie. You didn't brush your hair."

Benny muttered a quick spell, and her hair sorted and tidied itself, wrapping up into a professional bun.

"Much better, darling. He has been waiting all day. There was an omen yesterday, and he has been eager to speak with you."

Benny hugged her mother and headed to the study. The door opened and closed silently as she entered the largest collection of magical books in the state, possibly the country.

Her father was leaning over his work desk and eyeing a vial of blue liquid.

He looked up and smiled. "Ah, Beneficia. I am glad that you made it before heading out tonight. Drink this."

She took it and tossed it back. "What was that?" The taste left on her tongue was hot strawberries and fungus.

Benny handed him the vial, and he tucked it onto a rack next to four other doses of the same liquid.

"It is a protection and concealment spell. I also want you to take the charm that your uncle Magnus left you."

She winced. "It is so heavy."

"There was an omen last night. Something is stirring around you, Beneficia. Your safety might be in the hands of the XIA, but they do not know what you are. They can't guess at how valuable you could be in the wrong hands."

Benny sighed, and she went to her section of the library. The shelves were filled with some of the most powerful charms ever crafted, and they were all hers. Each one was given to her on a birthday or graduation. The charm that her uncle Magnus had given her was the size of her open hand, but at least it was flat. The weight she hated was actually the magical protection that coated her skin.

She found the case and opened it, sighing as she draped the chain around her neck and settled it under her shirt.

"There we go, Dad. Happy?"

He smiled, his bright eyes tired. "I will be happier when I know that you are safe."

"Would you feel better if I didn't go on this assignment?"

"No, it has nothing to do with where you are. Something is coming for you, and it doesn't matter where you are or who you are with. Some events cannot be avoided."

Benny blinked at the sober look on his face. "You are really worried."

He came over and stroked her cheek. The magic of her defenses crackled.

"I am very worried. I have been fielding calls all day. All of your aunts and uncles with a bit of precognition are worried about you."

She blinked. That was a lot of magical academics. Her childhood had been filled with folk she called aunt or uncle who were unrelated to her. Her family consisted of a long line of only children.

"I will be extra careful. I promise. You know me; I am not going to do anything stupid."

He smiled. "I know that you are careful, but when this kind of darkness pursues you, you have to meet it head on with as much armament as you can muster. Once we know what we are up against, we can create a battle plan."

"Like at Easter?" The long-standing making of maps of the grounds and segmenting the areas for maximum egg retrieval never failed to frustrate her mother's attempts to make it challenging.

Her father laughed. "Exactly like Easter. Now, your mother has some dinner for us. Let's go."

He offered her his arm, and she took it out of long habit. They left the library and followed the scent of one of her mother's dinners. Benny wished that she had inherited the cooking gene, but she would have to be content with the ability to find food.

Before they tucked into the meal, she asked her dad, "Why do I still taste strawberries?"

Her mother portioned out the mashed potatoes. "It is to cover up the taste of troll, Beneficia. It was one of the strongest flavours we could find."

Benny swallowed and reached for her glass of juice. She gulped it and put it down. "For future reference, nothing covers up the taste of troll."

Her mother chuckled and her father grinned. It was a normal family dinner at the Ganger house.

She pulled Pooky into the parking lot and locked it behind her while she hustled to the vehicle where her team was waiting for her. "Sorry. Am I late?"

They stood in their dark uniforms and badges, smiling.

Tremble chuckled. "We were afraid we had scared you off yesterday."

Argyle smiled slowly. "If you are ready, we will go."

Smith moved around and opened her door for her. "I have been ready to go for an hour."

Benny rolled her eyes and settled into the SUV with her notepad and pen at the ready.

They climbed in with Smith at the wheel and Argyle on the computer. They really did take turns.

Tremble was next to her, and they left the parking lot with a smooth glide of the wheels.

Day two was underway.

Chapter Five

Breaking up bar fights was not normally an XIA duty, but when it was a newly transformed stone giant causing the fuss, it definitely called for additional help for the bouncers.

Benny stared at the familiar logo of Syren's Karaoke Club. It was not the sort of place that she had ever seen a giant before.

"Stay in the car, Benny." Tremble muttered it on his way out.

"No. Witnessing this is within my agreement. I just have to stay out of the danger zone, which is about twenty feet for a giant. I won't get that close, but I need to see how you guys handle these situations."

"Twenty feet?"

"Yes. Twenty feet away." She smiled.

He watched the flow of traffic out of the club and jerked his head. "Stay safe."

She followed him into the club and stuck to the wall. This was her hangout on weekends with Freddy and a few other friends.

When she eased into the main room, she could see the problem. The giant had a group of partiers pinned up against the stage, and the XIA agents were joining another team in surrounding him.

She watched as one attempt from the other team failed. Claws didn't work. Strength didn't work and magic bounced off. Benny wondered how they were going to solve this and stayed as close to the wall as she could. When the giant spotted her, a light came to his eyes.

"Sing!"

Benny blinked. "What?"

"You! Sing!" He pointed right at her.

She squinted at his features and tried to see the human that had been inside him. "Holy shit."

Her mind pasted a picture of a young, gangly man who participated in every week's competitions and who enjoyed nothing more than to sit and listen to song after song warbled by other contestants.

He brought his fist down on a table shattering it to chunks. "Sing!"

Kobar was crouched near the precious equipment, and he waved at her. "What do you want, Benny?"

"Bring me life."

Argyle nodded slightly, and Benny took that as permission. She stayed out of the smashing range and eased up onto the stage.

Kobar handed her the mic and brought up the music and display. She didn't need it. She knew this one song backward and forward.

The lyrics began slowly as the song explained a normal human existence and the longing to be exceptional.

Benny watched, and the giant turned toward her, lumbering to the foot of the stage.

She sang about waking up in a body that wasn't hers. Breaking her mirror because she had become something new, something dangerous that she couldn't accept.

The agents got the hostages out.

The song changed to accepting the magic that had lodged inside and the new family, new friends and new life, which blossomed out of the change.

The giant looked at her dreamily, and Benny put as much of her inner siren as she could into that song.

Another officer rushed in on silent feet with headphones. Argyle and Tremble took the headset and eased up to the giant just as the song was ending. The man shook himself out of his stupor and yelled, "Sing."

She turned to Kobar. "Bring me the power."

He swiftly moved his hands over the keyboard and the song roared to life. Benny didn't like singing it first, but it should to a good job of disguising what the officers were up to.

She was halfway through the first chorus when they got the headphones on him. Pure siren song locked him in his own mind, and he fell backward with a tremendous thud.

Benny waved at Kobar, and he cut the music. She put the mic down and crept out to the SUV while the others bodily hauled the giant out of the club.

Smith was the first one back to the car, and he handed her a bottle of water. "I think you need this. You did well. He might have hurt someone before the headset arrived if you hadn't been there. How did he know you could sing?"

She sipped at the water. "Before his change, he was a regular at the club. He would sing and he had an okay voice, but he would listen to each and every performer. I hang out there on the weekends, and he recognised me."

"And you recognised him."

"It took some doing. He must have had a latent shift some time in the last month or so." She remembered the look in his white eyes and shivered.

"His community officer will deal with him at the station. For now, we got him under control and no one got hurt."

She looked at the heavily armoured collection van and the four men carrying the giant between them. "I am glad no one got hurt, but he is still trying to fit himself back into the human world. He is in for a rough time."

The others returned to the vehicle, and Argyle's fingers moved rapidly over the computer terminal while they all settled in.

Tremble smiled at her. "You have a good voice."

She swallowed more water and nodded. She had pitched her voice to enthral the giant, an old siren's trick that she had gotten from one of her great grandparents. Her dad was right; her life was suddenly getting dangerous.

Her blend of magic could be explained, but not all in the same body.

She sat back and quietly noted the next few stops. They checked on some apothecaries and then drove off to arrest an unlicensed precog who was selling slivers of the future.

The young man looked at the officers with contempt, right up until the point where Smith put the cuffs on him. Fear trickled through his expression.

That draining of colour got her attention. He didn't seem inclined to share his information with Smith, but with her father's warning in her mind, Benny wanted to know.

She angled to intercept him as he was led to the transport. "What did you just see?"

He leaned back and stared at her. He got a sly look in his eyes. "Why should I tell you?"

"Because I know something that you don't about your skills."

He snorted. "I can see the future."

The officer holding him raised his eyebrows in an indication to make it fast.

"Tell me what you saw and I will tell you what might get you out by the end of the evening."

The young man mulled it over for a second before leaning forward and whispering in her ear. Benny kept her face impassive, which turned into a grin when he touched his cheek to hers.

He blinked. "What the hell?"

She laughed. "I am warded against casual intrusion. Now, when you get to the agency, ask them to test you for seer focus. That is all you need to do."

"What?"

"Your talent for foresight is directional. You have options for your vision, and you are choosing the most traumatic."

He blinked. "How do you know that?"

"It is a natural instinct in your kind. You want to see the worst in order to prepare for it. Unfortunately, you charge people for what you see and that is what has gotten you into this situation."

"My kind?" He looked both intrigued and offended.

"Human seers. So, ask them to test you for seer focus. It can't hurt, and it might keep you from being arrested." She waggled her eyebrows.

He frowned and headed to the transport with the officer behind him.

When Benny turned toward the SUV, her agents were all lined up and watching her. "What?"

Smith grinned, "Is there something you want to tell us?"

"Yes, Argyle needs to drive for the rest of the night." She sighed. "I will explain more in the car."

Smith looked at Argyle. "I am okay with it if you are."

Argyle shrugged. "Sure. But you get to do double tomorrow and Thursday."

They shook on it, and everyone resumed their position in the vehicle.

When Argyle had pulled away from the curb, Smith turned to her. "So?"

"He saw an accident in which we get a spike through the window on the driver's side. Argyle could survive the damage, you couldn't. Argyle also has faster reflexes, so we probably won't get into the accident anyway."

Argyle looked up to the rear-view mirror. "Thanks for that."

She smiled. "If you are injured, you can use me for repair."

Benny could swear that he licked his lips, but she *knew* that he winked as the next call came in.

Smith gave the address to Argyle, and they were on their way.

The location was a cemetery, and flares of magic had been felt, but the magic users at the dispatch centre had determined that the magic wasn't human. It meant the XIA had to come in.

Argyle opened his window and shut the lights down as their vehicle glided on the paved pathway of the Heartway Cemetery.

"What are we doing?" She whispered it to Smith because Tremble was focussing, his hands cupped in front of him.

"Tremble is looking for the source of the energy pattern."

Argyle cruised through the dark space between the glowing white and grey stones.

Tremble opened his hands, and a small orb of light floated up and toward Argyle. The light moved to the left side of the steering wheel.

At the next turn, they went left.

They cruised through a number of turns, and finally, the light lowered. Argyle stopped the vehicle, and a number of hand signals went through the car. Benny could barely make them out; her night vision was her one weak point.

They slipped out of the car, and she took the hint and stayed inside the vehicle.

With no one around her, she reached out with her own senses and picked up on the crackling energy of a communication spell. Someone was trying to talk to a dead person and that person was not using human magic; there was the definite taste of trees in the air.

The spell was interrupted, leaving a lot of power hanging in the air.

Benny made notes as she felt what was going on with the change of attitude in the energy. She finally gave in to her curiosity and followed the power signature out of the vehicle to the group standing around and discussing communicating with the dead without a permit.

Tremble came to stand next to her. Benny whispered, "Is she going to drain the spell?"

He cocked his head. "She said she did."

"It is still here. I was top of my class in spell identification. The power is in the air."

Tremble nodded. "Right. Well, I will speak with her."

Tremble went to speak with the woman who was obviously a dryad. The woman got angry and the power surged.

The grass on the grave that she had set the spell on began to grow rapidly.

Tremble and Smith held her. Argyle called out. "Benny, is there anything you can do?"

She sighed and approached the grave while the woman shrieked and fought with the strength of an ancient oak.

The headstone was that of a man who died in his early forties. He was either a son or a lover. Either way, his connection to her was his link to the world.

The spell was simple and had a few ingredients. Benny took the water vessel that had been left on the grave and scooted all the energy back together, embedding it in the water.

Benny stood and turned to face the furious dryad. "Gentlemen, let her go."

The woman lunged, and Benny struck her with the water of her own power. She was overwhelmed and passed out.

Benny sighed and broke up the small items that she had needed to fire off the spell. All were readily available within twenty metres of the grave, so it wasn't destroying vital evidence.

Tremble eyed her as Smith and Argyle cuffed their catch.

"How did you do that?"

"Simple spell cancelling. I put the power into the water and threw the water at the dryad. She is tree based, and her skin absorbs water on reflex." Benny got to her feet, dusting her hands off.

"How did you know how to do that?" Tremble walked back toward the SUV with her.

"Practice. I did take spell work at university. I just happened to major in journalism." She smiled.

"I am guessing that your transcripts from school would make for fascinating reading."

She shrugged as the lights of the transport approached. "They were part of the reason I am here on this ride-along."

"That and your knack for recipes."

"How could I possibly forget?" Benny laughed and got back in the SUV.

Chapter Six

When the accident came, the SUV spun to the side as the pipes shot through the driver's side and pierced Argyle.

The vehicle that had lost its load of pipes was stopped a few feet away, and Smith was staring at the end of the metal that would have ended his life.

Argyle hissed. "Get me out of here."

Smith called the emergency services, and Tremble got out of the vehicle.

He grabbed for a kit in the back of the vehicle and came around the side. Benny went out his door; hers was pinned by the same pipes that were running through Argyle.

Smith was out of the SUV, and he had the driver pinned to the vehicle while he watched Tremble hacksaw off the following edge of tubing.

Benny grabbed the window striker, and she crawled into the front seat where Argyle was holding terribly still. "I am just going to break the window so we can get you away from the door."

He nodded slightly. She struck the window, and the glass shattered into a sheet that folded when she pushed at it with her forearm.

The object had entered below his arm and punched down to the spot just above his hip. The blood was dripping sluggishly, but he could survive it. Smith would have had no chance.

Tremble sliced through the outer pipe and reached inside to make quick work of the inner section. The moment that he was free, Tremble came around and pulled Argyle out of the vehicle through the passenger side.

Without saying anything, Argyle pulled the pipe out of his body and threw it to clatter on the street.

Benny was a woman of her word. She offered her arm, and he bit down without hesitation. Her protection amulet heated, but it responded to ill will and bodily injury. It would stop Argyle if he got carried away.

Her head spun after a few minutes, but thankfully, the emergency services arrived with bags of blood for him.

She tapped on Argyle's cheek, and he looked at her. "They have blood for you, Argyle. Let go or I will make you let go."

He slowed his draw on her skin and released her forearm from his deadly grip.

Smith took her by the arm and licked the wounds closed once again.

"Thanks for asking about that warning."

She smiled and swayed. "Sorry, I am a little dizzy. He took quite a bit."

"I think you need something to eat, and our group is done for the night. The car is totalled." He smiled and put his arm around her.

"I have blood on me."

"Well, you were fairly close to him. It is natural for you to have blood on you."

She touched her ribs. "Nope. My blood. Can I see a medic please?"

Tremble must have been listening, because he grabbed her and carried her to the medics who examined the graze along her ribs. The young woman smiled. "It is a small cut. Two stitches. May I?"

Smith stepped forward. "I can heal her without the stitches. I would have if my partner hadn't hauled her off."

The medic raised her hands and stepped away. "Go ahead. I will be nearby if you need help."

Smith knelt at her side. "I know this wasn't covered in your authorisations, so may I?"

She looked into his eyes and nodded. "Yes, please. This isn't really comfortable."

Benny held the shirt away from her skin and left the area clear. Tremble moved behind her and took over holding the fabric as well as pulling her against him to support her.

She leaned back, and when she was comfortable, Smith leaned forward and applied his tongue to her wound. She wouldn't have said that an alpha would be out as an XIA operative, but only the alphas gained the ability to heal. It was a means of keeping the other shifters subservient. They had to surrender to the alpha in order to be healed.

When Smith applied his tongue to her, she tried not to hiss. He lapped around the edges and finally dragged the rough pad over her wound.

Tremble tried to distract her. "You know, the average young lady would not be so calm in the face of having a wound licked closed."

She gave him a narrow-eyed look. "You still think I am average? How sweet."

Smith chuckled.

Argyle came toward them and sat on the edge of the emergency vehicle with one blood bag clamped in his jaws and two more in his hand.

Benny looked at him. "Oh shit. I forgot. How are you doing?"

He grinned—a weird and bloody grin, "I am doing well. Your immediate help was invaluable."

She could see him sparkling with energy and hoped that he came down from his high before he tried to drive or before he lifted the SUV from the wreckage.

Smith kept lapping at her skin, and she shivered. The pain was gone, and the healing had turned to a hot wave of interest that got the attention of all three men with her.

She blushed. "Sorry about that. That particular area is a bit sensitive."

Smith dragged his tongue along her skin, but when she realised he was outside the scope of her injury, she grumbled and flicked a finger against his forehead. "I am not an all-day sucker. If there is no more wound, you can stop now. Thank you for your help."

He sighed and ran his tongue across her one final time before lowering her shirt back into place. "That is the most fun I have had on shift in years."

Argyle grumbled. "Speak for yourself."

Tremble chuckled and helped Benny sit up. "It isn't the worst night we have had, but it does become one of the most memorable."

Benny sighed. "I am just glad that it didn't become a pissing contest when I mentioned what the seer had said."

Smith and Argyle shrugged. Smith said, "If it was true, it would save my life, and if not, I would just have to drive for the next two days."

Argyle shrugged and prepared to switch bags. "Driving isn't an issue for me. I don't mind, so it wasn't a big deal."

Tremble chuckled. "We aren't here because we are set in our ways. Each of us joined the XIA because we wanted to protect our communities and the extranatural community at large. We are flexible."

She blinked and tried to ignore the subtle invitation in his voice. "Right, well, what happens now? We obviously can't continue tonight."

Tremble looked at her with surprise. "Why not? A change of uniforms and a new vehicle and we are on our way."

"Seriously?"

Smith nodded. "Let's not be crazy, we will take a break and have dinner. But yeah, we keep going."

Benny wanted to go home and change her shirt, but that wasn't an option...or was it. "Can we swing by my house, so I can change my shirt?"

Argyle shrugged. "I don't see why not. Where do you live?"

"Anchor Lane. It's about ten minutes from here."

"Well, our ride just arrived, so we can get going as soon as I change." Argyle opened the buttons of his dark shirt and peeled it off.

Benny quickly found anywhere else to look. Argyle had been in amazing shape before he had become a vampire. He still had a golden tone to his skin over the grey base colour. The ridges of his abs were a work of art, and only the stripes of the injury marred the view.

He was oblivious to her admiration as he returned to their SUV where he grabbed a bag out of the back and he flicked out a new shirt.

"Pull your eyes back in your head, Benny." Tremble was amused.

She blushed hot and Smith laughed.

"Sorry. The extranormals I hang around with are usually not humanoid shaped. They tend to have extra limbs and such." She looked at her blood-stained hands. "Sorry."

Tremble put his hand on hers, and Smith echoed him.

Tremble said, "I did not mean to cause you any issue or embarrassment. I forget that humans are subject to that kind of thing."

She swallowed and nodded, trying to pretend that he was right in his assessment. He wasn't. She had been imagining pinning Argyle up against the SUV and having her way with him while the other two watched, but that was what happened when you had an alternative upbringing. The colour in her cheeks had been excitement.

Smith gave her a curious look, and she tried to put a frown on her face. This was the hardest part of being what she was; pretending to be what she looked like.

He helped her stand up, and she swayed.

They walked toward the new vehicle, and she locked up. "My notes, my bag."

Tremble patted her arm. "I will get them. You go and have a seat."

Smith kept supporting her until he was tucking her in the new vehicle that

Argyle was signing for. "You aren't what you seem, are you?"

She blinked. "What do you mean?"

"I have tasted magic users before, and while I taste magic in your blood, there is a whole lot more." His head bent toward hers, and the warm scent of him swamped her.

"Most girls are more than what they seem. You are reading more into me than there is."

"You are also skilled at evasion. That comes with practice. You are not saying no, but you are not saying yes. It is quite the dance."

She gave him a narrow-eyed look. "Why does it matter?"

"I am an investigator. I despise a mystery. I will solve you before this is over."

"Is that a threat?"

He grinned. "I am an excellent investigator."

Tremble brought all of the bags and equipment to the new SUV. The delivery woman grinned. "Take care of this one."

Argyle growled and moved the car seat back into a driveable position.

Their group settled in their new vehicle, and Argyle didn't move until she put on her seat belt.

"So, where am I going?"

"Seventeen Anchor Lane. It is a small house off the gravel drive. It is just off Aspen Parkway."

He nodded, and they were on their way to her house.

She was nervous. She had never had anyone over to the dower house, at least not anyone male. Jessamine was going to get into such a flap over this.

The door opened like it normally did when she approached, but today, she had three XIA agents watching out for her.

"No, I swear it is fine, and I live alone for all intents and purposes." She tried to push through the wall of backs in front of her, but they insisted on clearing her house.

She thought it was just an excuse for them to rifle through her stuff.

Benny walked in and called out, "Hello, Jessamine."

Her companion came to her through the refrigerator. "Benny, did you know that there are men here?"

"Yes, I know. They are the XIA agents that I am shadowing for the week. When you opened the door, they used it as an excuse to charge in here."

"You look tired. There is something in your workroom for that."

She wrinkled her nose. "I will try to grab it if I have time. I need to change my shirt. I was in a bit of an accident."

Jessamine shot upward and then returned to Benny's side. "Two of them are in your bedroom. Shall I get them out?"

"Go ahead and spook them. I will be up in a moment."

Tremble was on the main floor, in the living room. Benny followed him.

"What are you looking at?"

"There are no pictures of you and your parents after puberty. You talk of them fondly, so I assume they are still alive."

Benny smiled slightly. "They are. I still see them nearly every day. They live just down the road."

"Why no pictures? They looked so blissfully normal."

She followed his gaze to the picture on the mantel with her parents cuddled together, her father's amber eyes smiling and her mother's brown eyes filled with love.

"They still look the same to me, but life isn't always kind. Anyway, you are on duty and I need to get Smith and Argyle out of my underwear drawer."

A shout sounded from upstairs followed by a thud.

Benny chuckled. "And that is my cue."

She sprinted upstairs while Tremble asked her if she kept mousetraps in her underwear. It didn't deserve a reply.

Chapter Seven

(J)essamine was guarding her lingerie, and the other two were standing back against her bed.

"Gentlemen, this is my housemate, Jessamine. Jessamine, the elf down-stairs is Tremble; this is Agent Smith and Agent Argyle. I will be down in a moment, guys. Shoo."

She flapped her hands at them, and the moment they were out, she opened her shirt, dropping it in the fireplace.

"What happened?"

"Car accident. Pipes punched through the car door. Argyle got the worst of it; I just got grazed."

"You are wearing a protection glyph."

"I am, but it protects against people, not hardware." Benny rummaged around and grabbed a dark-grey button-down shirt.

She quickly scrubbed her hands and headed back downstairs where the investigative team was analysing her photos and trophies.

"You have won several karaoke tournaments." Smith raised his brows in surprise.

"Yes. I cheated. Can we go now? I need to eat."

Tremble held up another. "Battle of the Bands?"

It was cheap, horrible and manipulative, but she began to shake, and she descended to the floor in a faint.

Argyle caught her before she made contact with the hardwood, and Jessamine flapped her hands.

"You have to get her something to eat. I would do it, but I can't touch anything around here. Well, not with witnesses around."

Benny fought a grin as she continued to fake weakness. It was Jessamine's greatest point of irritation that she could only be a poltergeist when there were no witnesses. When Benny was away, she could touch everything. The moment Benny returned, it was back to haunting only.

"There is some juice in the fridge. That should perk her up."

Benny glared at Jessamine through narrow eyes. Her mother made her freshly blended juices and stashed them in her fridge while she was gone. Drinking one would definitely perk her up, but she would be grossed out for hours.

The bottle of bright orange juice emerged with Smith sniffing it cautiously. Argyle sat her up, and she took the bottle with genuinely shaking hands. It was one of her favourites. Carrot, orange and ginger with just a hint of parsley. She was relieved to be able to actually get half the bottle down.

She shuddered slightly as she capped the bottle. "That should do."

She shifted to her knees before getting to her feet. Argyle stood and steadied her as he helped her back to the kitchen. She put the bottle in the nearly empty fridge with finality.

She inhaled and boomed out, "Everybody in the car! You can rifle through my house the next time you are in the neighbourhood."

Argyle grinned, "I had no idea you had a voice like that."

"They don't give those karaoke awards to just anyone." She chuckled.

She locked the house though it wasn't necessary. If threatened, Jessamine would remain invisible and beat the crap out of any intruder.

The night air was crisp, and it was past midnight. Benny could feel the wild magic building all around them. It was one of the selling points of Anchor Lane; the magic was heady and heavy all around them. The perfect place for spell work.

Smith inhaled sharply and glanced over at her. "The air is heavy."

"Very."

"Is it always like this?" He looked up at the waning moon.

"Of course not." She climbed into the SUV and buckled in. Benny smiled. "Normally, it is far stronger."

Argyle laughed and reversed out of her driveway before heading back to the parkway. "So, where shall we head next?"

They were on their way back to Demrah's taco stand when an urgent call came through. Benny made notes on the evening's activities until the radio crackled.

All XIA units in the area were asked to report, and Benny's note taking took on an urgency.

She saw the collection of vehicles accumulating near the park, and she swallowed nervously. The coroner's van was an indicator that this was not going to be an amusing anecdote for the blog.

The normally cheerful guys were solemn as they left the vehicle. She checked that her pass was clipped on her belt, and she eased out of the SUV and trailed behind them, staying outside the tape that had been hastily erected.

She put her hand over her mouth when the woman who was floating in the air suddenly dropped. It wasn't a woman anymore; it was a body.

Benny looked closely and watched for the departing spirit. There was nothing. She stared and frowned, concern growing. There should have been something. There should have been a soul.

She let her features go blank and went looking. Nothing. No whiff of a soul and a dark hole where it should have been. Whatever killed her did it by ripping her life force out and pulling it through her soul until the ragged piece left behind had gone with the flame of existence. First, her battery had been drained and then someone pulled the plug.

Benny watched her XIA agents mingle with others of their rank before they moved in an organised wave, seeking clues.

Benny crouched and focussed on the young woman. She was about Benny's age and was dressed for work.

There were no marks on her wrists or ankles or around her neck. Either whatever had taken her had convinced her to go along or it had sedated her with magic and transported her here.

The fact that she was dressed for work was strange. If she was out in the evening, she should either be in casual or party clothing. The suit and sensible pumps didn't match the passage of time. Even working overtime, she should have been home hours ago.

She watched the men meticulously picking up and bagging every bit of evidence after photos had been taken. She took note of the gloves that appeared from every pocket and the care with which the scene was examined. Lights were blazing bright, and the scene lit the park up. If the centrepiece had been anything other than a dead body, it would have been beautiful.

When the challenge came, it was from the coroner's people.

"Who are you?"

She stood and showed her badge. "I am a special observer with the XIA."

The young woman with the grey cast to her skin sniffed at her. "You smell like blood."

"There was a car accident earlier. I am sure that my jeans and shoes are covered in it."

"There is none on your shirt."

"I changed my shirt, but I had three XIA agents rifling through my living room, so I left it at that. Tomorrow, I will bring a full change of clothing, though I have no idea where I would change."

The woman suddenly smiled. Benny jerked back in shock. The medic assistant went from a cold vampire to a stunning woman. The transformation was reversed when the woman resumed her calm face and headed to where the coroner was examining the body and checking the temperature.

Argyle spoke from next to her. Benny jumped again; she hadn't heard him approach. She was just not on her game today.

"She is the mayor's new assistant."

"A new vampire?"

"Oh, she isn't a vampire...not yet. She is his assistant."

"But she has the same presence I am used to in vampires."

He grinned, his fangs flashing. "I know, but Miss Wicks is still in possession of a beating heart. She appears when there is something that he needs to concern himself with."

The woman in question returned. "It was pleasant meeting you, Beneficia Ganger. Agent Argyle, there will be a mage team going over this place with seers. Make sure that it isn't compromised."

He nodded. "Yes, Miss Wicks."

The woman pulled her calm face into a grimace and stuck out her tongue.

Benny chuckled. "It was nice to meet you, Miss Wicks."

"Call me Leo. It is short for Leonora. I am sure I will see you again, Miss Ganger."

She didn't say good night as she walked away. Benny looked at the body and knew why.

"We are going to be stuck here for the rest of the night. Did you want to catch a ride back with the coroner?"

Benny looked over at the body and nodded. "If they wouldn't mind."

She needed to get a little closer to the woman to determine where the soul had been ripped out, but if she was actually a human, there shouldn't be any way for her to know that the soul was missing. No one had mentioned it, but the coroner would figure it out. They were usually in the undead spectrum, and locating souls was part of their business.

Argyle asked the coroner's assistant, and she nodded and spoke quickly.

Argyle came back. "You will have to ride with the body bag in the back."

"That is fine. I am really exhausted by the events of the night. Some peace and quiet in the back of the van won't hurt me."

He gave her a piercing look, but didn't comment.

Benny winced as she realised that she should be upset at the thought of sharing space with a dead woman. Dang, she really was tired.

She waited while the preliminary exam was made and the woman was bagged up. When the gurney was tucked away, the assistant beckoned to Benny, so Benny waved good night to the others.

She settled in the back of the van, introduced herself to the assistants who were in the only two seats in the vehicle, and she looked at the body bag, closing her eyes as she looked for hints of magic or other energies.

"I apologise for the lack of seating, but we don't often transport the living." The woman smiled shyly.

"It is fine. I was just thinking that she looked so normal. Like she had just left work."

The passenger turned more fully to her. "I know. It is usually difficult to see them like that. The lack of blood is disturbing though."

"I didn't see any wounds."

"There aren't any. That is what is so weird. Did you want to sit in on the autopsy?" The young woman was eager. She wasn't a vampire, wasn't a zombie. Benny guessed ghoul, but it was impolite to ask.

"Molly, that is up to Dr. Tanner." The driver sighed.

"He will say yes. I promise." The young ghoul smiled widely, showing a tremendous array of yellowed fangs.

"I would love to if he authorises it."

Molly beamed and turned to face the dashboard. "He will."

Benny kept her senses running across the body next to her for the rest of the ride. She really doubted that she would be allowed in the autopsy room.

Chapter Eight

$\mathcal{B}$enny put on the disposable tunic and the facial shield as well as the rubber gloves and booties. Dr. Tanner had said yes.

It was unusual for a zombie to show this level of animation, but Dr. Tanner waved his arms and explained every point in the process.

They began by photographing every inch of the woman before they undressed her, putting the clothing into evidence bags. Dr. Tanner looked for any unusual markings, and he was thorough, examining her from the toes up. When he finished his visual examination, he took a few photos of the area around her mouth.

He and his assistant turned her over, and they examined her back. With his fingers, he parted the hair, and there must have been something there, because he shaved the back of the head.

"Found it. She was branded. Get that camera around here."

The assistant handed Dr. Tanner the camera, and the doctor went to work.

"Miss Ganger, come here and look at this." He smiled and pointed out the icon that had been burned into the scalp.

"Why wasn't it visible before?"

"My guess is that it was applied after she had been levitated. They flipped her over, lifted her hair, marked her and then put her back and drained her. You can see here on her mouth that she had some internal bleeding. Whatever removed her soul also took her blood."

Benny blinked innocently. "Removed her soul?"

"Yes, we usually see that sort of thing in demon attacks, but there hasn't been one of those in the city for fifteen years, and the demons don't take blood. This is something new."

Dr. Tanner went to work opening the woman up, but there was no blood. All the organs revealed were pale, and it was exceptionally sad.

Benny watched the autopsy, and he completed his findings of soul death by magical means by person or persons unknown.

She swayed and remembered that she had lost a lot of blood and hadn't had anything to eat all night. Benny excused herself and headed for the parking lot and her car.

Pooky did most of the driving, but he didn't take her home, he took her to her parents' house with the sun trumpeting noon above her.

Benny stumbled into the hall and headed for the library. Her father lifted his head from his desk, and she raised her hand. "Soul consumption with branding and blood consumption."

Three books came soaring out of the stacks and landed on her desk.

"Benny, what happened?"

"A woman is dead in the park, no soul; it was scooped out like a melon, and then, some son of a bitch drained her blood after he branded her."

"Can I help?"

"They think it might be a demon attack, so you can help me look."

Benny grabbed a pen and paper; she drew the glyph carefully, leaving an opening in the mark in case it had the power to summon.

She and her father went through the huge tomes, page by page, atrocity by atrocity.

Her mother came in with a tray and cleared her throat. "Enough!"

They both looked up. Her father gave his wife a slow smile of welcome.

"What is it, Mom?"

"Benny, you need to eat, and if you are going back to work tonight, you need to change your clothing. Jessamine brought some clothes over earlier. Take a shower, eat and drink this tonic. It will keep you going until morning. You know how you get with no sleep."

"I need to find this, Mom."

"So, let me and Dad look. You go and refresh yourself. I made your favourite. Cream tea."

Benny stepped away from the demonology tome. "Fine. But there had better be a chocolate tart in there or I will be cranky."

Her mother let her go, but Benny heard, "How will I be able to spot that with your normal cheery demeanour?"

"I heard that!"

Benny was on the stairs when she heard, "You were meant to!"

Benny ran up to her old room, and the folded fabric was sitting in the centre of her bed, right down to sneakers.

She got into the shower as fast as she could, hoping that the rush of water would drown out the sound of her father and mother having a quickie. It was in his bloodline, just as it was in Benny's, and her mother was remarkably tolerant of both of them.

Her parents' physical needs were one of the primary reasons for her moving out. There were some things that defied explanation to a date or one's girl-friends.

She noted the pink tinge to the water and guessed that she had been wearing more blood in her clothing than she thought. It was hard to tell, both her jeans and the vampire blood had been black.

When she was warm, clean and definitely refreshed, she wrapped herself in a towel and scrubbed at her hair. It felt good to be home; everything was where it was supposed to be. She brushed her hair out and whipped it into a ponytail before she put on her underwear and the jeans and t-shirt.

The shoes were her favourites and not at all appropriate for being with the XIA. They were white, silver, blue and had a streak of pink that tied the look together. Benny really hoped that she wasn't going to step in any blood tonight.

She trotted down the stairs to the library with her protective charm between her breasts again.

Her parents were decent, but the windows were open and the candles were burning. Telltale signs of their recent intimacy.

Her mother had one of the tomes in front of her, and she tapped her finger. "I found it, and it isn't good. Now, Benny, eat."

The table in the centre of the room was set with tea and the three-tiered tray full of sandwiches and treats.

"Can you read it out loud while I eat?"

"Of course."

Benny went over and kissed her mother's cheek before she scampered over to the tea.

Her mother intoned the description of the ritual, and finally, she set up the important bit, it was an exorcism for soul transfer, but it would only work with a demon soul.

Benny paused with a salmon sandwich at her lips. "Demons don't have souls. That is what makes them demons."

"That is what it says. This is to be used if you have a demon with a soul and you want to sell the soul as a commodity. It has to have happened before or this spell would not be here."

Benny nodded and ate her narrow sandwich with as much enjoyment as she could. She went for the blueberries with clotted cream next.

With deliberate focus, Benny made her way through the tower of sandwiches, cakes and tarts. No bad news was going to put her off her love of the teeny sandwiches.

She sat back with her tea, and her mom reached into her apron, withdrawing two vials. One was the blue protective vial and the other was the energising vial. Benny made a face. "You couldn't have reminded me before I ate the last cream puff?"

Her mom smirked. "No. I need to get my fun where I can."

Benny got up and took the vials. "I still love you, Mom."

"Not for the next ten minutes, but I know your heart is in it."

Benny gulped the energiser first, shuddered and gagged, and then scarfed down the enhanced identity protection potion. Strawberries and fungus. *Yum.*

As fast as she could, she returned to the table and slugged down her Earl Grey Tea.

She poured another cup and scooped honey into it, drinking the hot mix as fast as she could. The flavour lingered, and she prayed that she didn't start belching.

Benny faced her parents across the room. "Now, who would want to pull a soul that wasn't a demon? Why did they kill that woman?"

Her father shook his head. "That is what the XIA has to investigate."

Benny sighed. "Abiding by the law is hard."

"Oh, sweetie, you are only beginning to understand. You have lived your life as a human, and I am delighted that you could, but there are prejudices out there that extranormals are all subject to, and your family bloodlines blend most of the dangerous races. How you ended up looking so human is a blessing that your mother passed along; it certainly didn't come from my side of the family."

She looked at her father and sighed. His sacrifice had put him in a situation of house arrest. Their friends and family came to them, and it was those tolerant people that had given Benny her start in life. Now, she was dealing daily with those who had not faced that kind of threat to their existence because of their appearance. They just didn't understand.

Benny was in her car and heading for the agency when her phone rang. She pulled over at the side of Anchor Lane and answered. "Hello?"

"Benny? This is Tremble. There has been another victim and the pathologist has seen some demonological symbols."

She cleared her throat. "Really?"

"Yes, the expert refused to meet with the day shift, so we are on our way there. He is located on Anchor Lane, so I thought we could pick you up this evening."

She looked toward her house. "Um, sure, when will you be here?"

"We are just pulling onto Anchor Lane."

"See you."

She dropped her phone and quickly drove forward to park her car. She threw her bag with her soiled clothing into the house and took the duffel that Jessamine had prepared for her. A moment later, she was waiting for them as they pulled into her drive.

She hopped into the car. They all looked a little the worse for wear. "Where are we going?"

"Thirteen Anchor Lane. Your neighbour. Apparently Dr. Emile is the local expert on demonology."

She fought the urge to cover her eyes. "Yes, I have heard that."

They drove to her family home, and she got out of the car with them. The agents put themselves between her and the unknown. *How sweet.*

Argyle knocked on the door, and Benny watched her mother open it.

"Good evening, madam. We are here to speak with Dr. Emile. We are agents with the XIA."

Her mother spotted her. "Beneficia dear, go make some tea. I will show them into the library."

"I will make the tea after they meet Dad." Benny weaseled between them and beckoned them inside. "Please come in."

Once everyone was inside the foyer, Benny made the introductions. "Agents Tremble, Argyle and Smith, this is my mother, Lenora Ganger. Dr. Lenora Ganger, master magus."

The men greeted her mother, but they were looking at her like she had grown another head.

Benny led them to the library, and she paused to let them take in her father's emerald skin, the wide curving horns, slit pupils in his amber eyes and the claw-like nails at the end of his fingertips.

"Agents Tremble, Argyle and Smith, this is my father, Dr. Harcourt Emile Ganger."

Tremble looked at her. "Your father was human."

She rocked her hand. "He was. Sort of. It is a long story. I will go and make the tea."

Benny escaped the library with a whoosh of relief.

Her mom was nearby. "You did well. Very professional. They had no idea?"

"They might have. Two out of three have tasted my blood." She blinked, shook her head and made her way to the kitchen.

The water boiled in two minutes, and she carried the tray of steeping tea into the library. Her mom brought another tray of sandwiches.

The agents were still standing at a distance from her father. She set the tray down on the table and went to hug her dad. He held her carefully as he always did. "Do you need anything, Benny?"

"Just a hug. I was so busy before I didn't hug you hello."

"Missed you, too, Benny."

When Benny turned, the agents had relaxed, and she gestured to the tray. "We found out why he did what he did. The ritual requires some explanation. Have a seat."

Confronted by her family, they sat.

The agents were silent. All three stared at her father as if he was a spectre.

Benny rubbed her forehead. She looked at her dad and he nodded. "Gentlemen, do you want me to explain?"

Argyle nodded. "Please."

Her dad picked up one of the tomes and kept flipping through the pages so they could stare at him without feeling awkward.

"Fine. My great grandmother was a succubus summoned to bear the heir of a wizard. That would be my grandfather. Once she had completed her contracted obligation to bear a human-looking heir, she returned to the demon zone. My grandfather grew up, married a were-wolf and had a son. He became a professor of arcane studies, and at the turn of the last century, he met my mom."

Her mother went over and wrapped her arms around her emerald mate. "It was love at first sight on my part, but his nose was so stuck in his books, I had to peel down to my corset and chemise before he would look my way."

Her father laughed. "And at that point, I could not look away."

Benny rolled her eyes and continued. "They got married and lived happily with my father and mother sharing their lives and their interest in magic. Mom aged slowly and her pregnancy with me took six years. She says it was worth it for the stares alone. Anyway, when I was ten, my mother got cancer. She was dying and she was doing it quickly."

Benny watched her dad put his arm around his wife protectively. She cleared her throat to get rid of the emotional wobble and sighed. "He waited until the moment she died, and he healed her body then transferred his human soul into her before she could completely pass on. They now share the one soul, but it was all that was keeping my father's parentage from being really obvious."

Smith cocked his head. "So that makes you part demon?"

Benny wrinkled her nose. "Well, not that it matters, but given my parentage and ancestors, I am really only one part human. The rest is a much longer story, and we have a killer to catch."

Her father slammed the tome shut and nodded. "Now that introductions and explanations have been made, let's get to work. This is time sensitive."

Chapter Nine

Tremble was staring at her with intense focus. "You are not human?"

She lifted the book with the initial explanation of the ritual and opened it to the ritual. "No. I look human, but that is a trick of my genes. If you look at my mom's ears, you can see the point and a slight ridge from a siren ancestor; there are signs of troll and fey around her. I think there is even some shifter in there."

Argyle wandered over and looked at the books. "I can't read that."

She pinched the bridge of her nose. "You can't. There are reasons that few people are capable of being demonology experts. Demon blood is a requisite for being able to read the script. I will translate if you like, or my dad can do it."

Her father grinned, flashing his deadly and shark-like teeth.

Smith nodded. "We trust your translation, Benny. Please proceed."

She squinched her eyes shut for a moment and then began. "All right. Well, the suspect is looking for a demon, a very specific demon."

Argyle was suddenly all business. "What demon?"

"A demon with a soul. The question is why that woman?"

Smith lifted his head. "She isn't the first. She is the seventh woman born on the same day to be killed in that particular way. The others were out of our jurisdiction, so it took most of the day to find them. The ladies were all the same age, within one week."

Benny whirled when she heard her father growl. "No."

Her mother placed her hand on his, but he continued to flex his muscles in agitation and the fan-like crest rose out of his dark hair.

Tremble whispered, "What is he doing?"

Benny scowled. "He is angry, but I don't know why."

Through clenched teeth, her father asked, "All born here thirty years ago in the ninth month on the twenty-third day, give or take?"

Her mother gasped. "Harcourt, you didn't!"

He nodded grimly. "I did. I mirrored Benny's soul on the other eight girls in the nursery."

Benny felt sick. "You have to be kidding."

Her father came to her and held her tight. "I wanted to protect you and that was the only way I knew how. Your power signature was distinctive, even when you were a baby."

Smith asked, "You are thirty? You don't look thirty."

The sound he made immediately afterward indicated one of the others had struck him.

"Why not just a shield?" She mumbled it against his chest.

"Magic is too noticeable. The other girls were all healthy with young parents, so the likelihood of them moving was strong."

"They died because of me."

His hand stroked her hair, and he murmured to her as he had when she was a teenager. "No. They died because someone is trying to kill you, or at least part you from what is rightfully yours."

"Ripping a soul from a demon. Why would someone do that?" She let him continue to hold her. It was for his need and not hers. He could not defend her in the wide world, but he could offer her comfort here.

He sighed. "I do not know about other demons, but if they took your soul, you would have to attach yourself to a more powerful demon of the zone for protection. You would become a slave."

"We will not let that happen." Tremble's voice was determined.

Argyle pitched in. "Do you know who the other woman is?"

Benny eased away from her father. He shook his head.

She swallowed. "I can find her. If she is carrying a mirror of my soul, I can get a location."

Her mother nodded and got a map. She flipped it out on one of the long tables and moved around the room collecting scrying equipment.

Smith asked softly. "What is she doing?"

"She is setting up a search map."

Her mother laid out the tools and beckoned for her to come close. "All right, sweetie. First, you know what to do."

Sighing, Benny took the bucket that her mother handed her and walked away from the crowd. Throwing up before working was an important part of scrying. She literally had to be hungry in order to track her prey. Her mother's bloodline had some creepy hunters in it, and her talent for all magic came from the maternal side of the family. Raw energy and power came from her dad's ancestors.

Once she had completed her purge, she rinsed out her mouth, washed her hands and face, and she glared at herself in the mirror before coming to a conclusion. This was going to take a lot of power, so she was going to have to drop a minor bit of glamour that she had been using since she was in kindergarten.

It took more effort to pull the glamour off than it did to keep it in place, but she needed every bit of access to her soul in able to create the template to search for.

Her left eye glowed slightly and she sighed. The cat was out of the bag, the agents were going to see her as she was. Here was hoping that it didn't wreck the friendships she had been starting.

Benny kept her head high, but she was watching carefully for any signs of disturbance in the agents. There was a mild bit of blinking, but nothing major.

Smith quirked his lips. "You look a little pale."

She snorted. "Right. You see how you look when you have to puke on behalf of a tracking spell."

Tremble nodded as if he had figured it out, and Argyle sat still as stone.

Her mother had assembled all the implements, and she stood aside as Benny approached.

Benny closed her eyes and moved her hands over the assembled objects. Two items jumped into her hand. A heavy charm embossed with serpents and books joined a long black crystal bound with silver. Benny transferred them both to the same hand at the same distance from her palm and she exhaled slowly.

The map was of the entire continent, and she would work in narrowing areas until she pinpointed the target.

She held the pendants out and watched them pull from one side to the other as she focussed on herself. Both located her hometown, so Lenora moved the large map aside and pulled out one with local streets and surrounding areas.

When the pendants pulled toward her home, she blocked that and continued to move her hand until there was a second indicator. She followed the new location to a charming suburb.

Her mother subbed out the maps again for a satellite view, and Benny focussed and indicated a house on the left side of a cul-de-sac.

"Bowl and knife." Benny kept her focus, and when her mother put the small bowl on top of the house image, Benny cut her finger and dripped six drops into the bowl. The blood swirled and took form.

"Jennifer Langstrom. Nineteen Yarrow Path." Benny staggered back, and her father helped with the first aid.

The agents were staring at her. She stared back. With her eye unglamored, she could see them for what they were, and it was an interesting sight.

Smith's body had a healthy golden glow, his hair nearly waved in the energy he was putting out, Argyle's eyes were sunken and his skin was chalky, but sparking with light from the inside out, and Tremble was a confusion of power and nature. His power was going in all directions all the time.

Smith blinked slowly. "Is your eye going to stay like that?"

She lifted her hand toward her face and could see the reflected light. "I am sorry, but it is. I can't put it away and then whip it out when I need it."

Out of reflex, she lifted the scry bowl to her lips and drank the water and blood drops. Tremble made a face, but the other two watched the bowl like it contained a treat.

Lenora tidied up. "Well, you have the address, you had better get going."

Smith paused. "Where did you get all those maps?"

Benny chuckled. "I will explain the idea of having friends on the planning committee, as well as being an official city archive in the car."

Tremble stiffened. "You cannot come along."

Benny crossed her arms. "I have to. There is no one else who can stop the spell work. It is an easy fix, but no one can manage it unless they have mage training with demon control as a primary field of study."

Argyle smirked. "You have studied it?"

Her father cleared his throat. "It was necessary. She had to use it for the first time when she was fifteen. She is very good at it."

The agents looked over at her father with his claws, bright eyes and evil fangs. They looked to her mother, and she merely smiled cheerfully.

"Benny is very good at doing what she feels is necessary. She isn't one to put herself in danger. She will keep herself as safe as she can." Lenora finished putting the maps away and neatly tidied the tools that had been used in the scrying.

Benny stood and drummed her fingers on her bicep with her arms crossed. "Jennifer is in danger right now. She was still at home, but I can track her if she is taken. Now that I know what I am looking for, she will leave a trail."

They nodded and took their leave of her parents. Benny was in the car and buckled up in under a minute and they were on their way to talk to Jennifer.

She wished that there was less silence in the car, and suddenly, there was.

"So, dating must have been awkward." Argyle chuckled.

Benny grinned. "You have no idea."

Smith chipped in, "Did you get asked out by normals?"

She wrinkled her nose. "Yes. Their families encouraged them because my parents were and are on the boards of five local universities. A relationship with me meant an increase in their choices for a higher education."

Two dates. She had had two dates before her father fully turned into what he was now. After that, all introductions to her parents had been short and to the point, and heavily glamoured. Glamour was hard to stick on a demon, but as long as her father stayed calm, he looked just like he used to.

Tremble cocked his head. "You introduced all of your prospective mates to your parents?"

She looked at him and raised her eyebrows. "You have met my parents; do you think I had a choice?"

The men in the car chuckled. Tremble grinned. "I suppose not. It must have made for a fascinating adolescence."

"That is one way of putting it. Mind you, in all those years of dating, I only had one bad experience." She chuckled.

Smith started to ask her about that one experience, but they arrived at Jennifer's home.

Tremble opened his door and looked at her.

Benny held up her hands. "I know. Stay in the car."

The agents left, and Benny kept her senses wide and looking for any signs of trouble.

Benny couldn't sense anything and that was when she got agitated. Jennifer was gone, and there was only the slightest hint of where she had been.

Chapter Ten

The moment the agents returned to the SUV, she said, "Down the block to the left."

The night air was cool and bracing, but Benny was stuck next to a closed window. She had to settle for the view she was getting through her mage's eye.

They were at the turning point in under a minute, and she tried to focus. "Okay, I am not trying to be difficult, but I can't sense her from inside the car."

Smith nodded. "Right. I am going to shift, and I will stay with you while you follow the trail."

They parked and left the vehicle. Tremble and Argyle were ready to move, but Smith had to strip.

Benny blushed and focussed her vision and senses on the trail left by her mirror.

The sound of flesh flexing, tendons snapping and claws scraping the pavement caused her to peek a little. Smith twisted and arched into his lion form, and he was huge.

The actual full shift of a shifter was always something that creeped her out. She could face anyone in a body that didn't conform to normal standards and see their true beauty, but the twist of a body from its natural state into another beast made her a little queasy. It was probably the snapping tendons and rippling flesh.

The lion came up to her and sniffed her, chuffing softly.

Argyle nodded. "He's ready. You are consulting here, but you are also observing. Do not involve yourself directly."

Benny focussed, and she started to run. The men were behind her, and Smith was at her side.

Jennifer was up ahead, and there was other magic, human magic, involved.

The faster they moved, the further away the soul seemed. Benny growled and started to run faster. The moment she got within a hundred yards, she felt the separation of soul and body. She grunted and put her power around the soul.

She staggered when something tried to crack through the protection. There was a shout of frustration, and heat was the next thing to strike her energy.

Benny and her followers burst through the hedges, and a horrifying sight greeted them.

A man wearing a shadowed cloak was hunched over the floating body of his victim.

Smith sleeked into an attack mode and charged the man.

Energy sparked as the pentacle halted Smith's advance.

Benny stumbled through the energy field and fought for air as she said, "Get away from her."

Confronting someone was not normally in her nature, but she could feel the pressure he was putting on her shields, and it was not comfortable. If she left him alone, he would crack through it and that would be the end of the woman in front of her.

The cowled head turned toward her. "Stay out of this, mage. You don't know what you are dealing with."

The agents were up against the warding and shouting at the attacker.

Benny stood straight and hit him with attacks spells she hadn't used in a decade. With her hands held a foot apart, she pelted him with balls of burning moonlight. The first few had no effect, but as she increased her speed, she knocked him away from Jennifer.

She kept firing at him, pushing him back toward the edge of his circle. If she could get him past it, the agents could get him.

Thud, thud, thud. The energy balls struck over and over until it was a solid stream of power that edged his foot into the circle.

The agents stumbled in, and the mage looked at her in shocked horror. "Bitch!"

A swirl of dark power wrapped him, and he disappeared.

Benny stumbled and shook her hands as the power had nowhere to go. It was time to put the soul back in the body.

Argyle looked at Benny. "What is wrong with her?"

She blinked, lifted her hands and grabbed the protective orb that she had cast. "Her soul is here, but she needs a healing before I put it back. Her body has been primed for blood loss. If I put her back in before the healers get here, she's dead."

Tremble was speaking on his phone, and he finished the call. "I called them when we first hit the barrier. They are driving in across the green."

He wasn't wrong. Benny could hear the approaching sirens and see the lights.

Smith came up behind her and supported her. She hadn't realised that she had been swaying. His lion form smelled of sunshine and musk. "Thanks, Smith."

He grunted and remained behind her while they waited for the healers to stabilise the victim.

Tremble marked out the transport site that the attacker had used. Argyle asked her, "Did you get a look at him?"

She nodded. "He was completely average with the exception of the twisted expression of greed and panic on his features."

"Could you describe him to an artist?"

Benny held out her hand, put an orb of energy into it and she printed the face from her mind onto the energy. "Here. Put this on some twigs and leaves and you can take a photo of it."

Tremble went to the shrubs and broke off a branch, bringing it back to carry the fey globe. "So, fey blood, too?"

"After this is over, I will invite you guys over and take you through the portrait gallery. The only thing I don't really have in me is a lot of normal human." She shrugged and eased the orb onto the leaves that would support it and give it energy for a few hours.

The medics started to load Jennifer onto a gurney.

Benny moved around Tremble. "Is she stable?"

"Non-responsive. We stopped the haemorrhaging. We will be able to treat her at hospital."

Benny nodded, grabbed the soul and she pushed it back into Jennifer's body without the mirroring of her own.

Jennifer started moaning and shifting, and the medics got into high gear.

Benny staggered backward, and Smith was there to support her.

Argyle caught her elbow and he frowned. "Are you all right?"

"I have just cast more magic in ten minutes than I have in ten years. I had forgotten what kind of an energy rush it is." She rubbed her forehead.

Tremble handed the orb over to some uniformed officers, and they carefully carried it to their vehicle before they taped off the scene.

Benny sighed. "What happens now?"

Argyle cocked his head. "You are interviewed, and we have to begin looking for the mage who was draining the victim."

She yawned and leaned against Smith, lounging on him as she lost focus. "Whomever is going to interview me had better work fast."

Another XIA vehicle pulled up, parking on the grass. The trio emerged up and stalked toward their team.

Argyle muttered, "I should get the SUV."

She reached out and grabbed his arm. "Not until I am sure that they are not going to arrest me."

He chuckled. "Right."

The three agents were cordial enough to her team, but Smith got a little bit of ribbing for his current shape.

The elf of their team, named Frond, brought out a notepad and smiled at Benny. "Now, can you tell us what you saw once you entered the circle?"

She explained the levitation, the man trying to drain the woman of her soul and his escape when she attacked.

"Are you a registered mage?" He raised a brow.

She blushed. "No. I am afraid I am home schooled. I am a registered mage guide, but that is about it."

He nodded. "You are that journalist that the XIA was asked to host."

"Correct. Benny Ganger."

He grinned. "I love your recipes."

"Thank you."

"What spells did you use to repel the assailant?"

"I used a moonlight repulsion spell in the form of rapid snowballs, and to protect Jennifer, I encased her psyche in a heavy warding with a starlight base and used my own body as a power source to maintain it."

He made frantic notes. "All mage-based?"

"Um, no. The light attack was fey. The protection was part mage and part fey." She smiled, and Smith rumbled behind her.

She took his sound to mean she should shut up.

"How can you master fey magic?" Frond raised his pale green brows.

"I never said I was a master; I said I was home schooled in magic. My parents are both academics. The books were all there."

He nodded and continued to make notes.

He opened his mouth to ask another question, but Smith shifted his position and pushed Benny away from the elf with his huge paw. He huffed and moved his head.

"You are kidding."

He made the motion again, and she boosted herself onto his back. Lion riding was not comfortable; they were made entirely of shoulder blade.

Her XIA team made their way back to their vehicle in silence. They all had been interviewed before being released.

At the SUV, Tremble helped Benny off her mount.

"Thanks, Smith."

He huffed and wandered around the vehicle before shifting back to human.

Argyle tucked her into the SUV and buckled her in place. "Call your parents. I managed to grab a soil sample for analysis. That power wasn't human, so it might give us a clue."

Benny sent her mother a text before she listed to one side as they started moving. Smith still tucking in his shirt. Tremble moved next to her and put his arm around her. "You did well, Benny. You saved a life tonight."

She gave a weak thumbs-up and drifted into a daze as they headed to her parents' home.

When they arrived, Argyle carried her out and into her family home.

Lenora came out and asked, "What is wrong with her?"

"She used a lot of energy tonight, and she has been weak since."

Her mother touched her cheek and looked Benny in the eye. With a rueful sigh, she touched Benny's neck and then jerked her hand sharply. "Rule one of spell casting, Benny?"

Benny felt her strength return in a rush. "Remove all protections and dampeners. Argyle, you can put me down now. I am an idiot."

Argyle held on to her for a few more moments until her father growled in the background.

Smith grinned. "You forgot to remove a dampener?"

She shrugged. "I wear one most of the time. I don't do magic in public, so it never occurred to me."

He chuckled. "Same reason I remove all the clothing. I can still shift, but it gets in the way."

Benny giggled and rubbed her arm against his in camaraderie.

Argyle took her left side and Tremble guarded her back.

"Mom, we got a soil sample from a transport site. It is less than an hour old, so there should still be something traceable."

Argyle handed the sample to her mother, and her father took it with a sharp plucking of his clawed fingers.

Benny's stomach growled. "Come on. While he works on that, I will make something to eat. You are still entitled to meals."

Her mother nodded with a smile and went into the lab with her father.

Benny led the other three to the kitchen and the huge butcher-block table. "Have a seat. Do you want something hot or cold?"

"Hot."

"Hot."

"Hot."

She chuckled and started a pot of water. "Soup it is."

They looked a little doubtful, but they remained quiet until the ingredients started to line the table while the water began to bubble. Their expressions turned to happy anticipation when she got the stock heating and the smell filled the kitchen. Her mother might do most of the cooking, but Benny was pretty fair when it came to feeding family and friends. She glanced at the attentive agents who were watching her with hope every time she touched ingredients. Yeah, they counted as friends.

Chapter Eleven

$\mathcal{T}$hey blinked at her as she set the huge empty bowls in front of them. Argyle looked a little nervous.

"Don't worry. My mom keeps a fully stocked pantry. Demon diets vary greatly depending on their exertions and the time of year."

Smith looked impressed.

The noodles were done and drained, so she divided the tangle into four large bowls and two clamp jars. The meat went on in layers, the vegetables went on next, herbs and finally the broth was ready to add to the bowls.

She kept Argyle's bowl to the side. It had the regular mix of meats plus some blood sausage. She went to the fridge and got the ceramic pitcher of blood, pouring a dollop into the bowl. Once that was done, she parcelled out the broth in the bowls and set out the chopsticks and spoons. The un-brothed clamp jars were tucked into the fridge for later.

A final touch was the selection of sauces, and she settled at the table with them. "Have at it."

She dug in and slurped at the noodles.

After a few seconds of hesitation, they all followed suit.

The slurping and flicking of broth was tremendous.

Smith blinked. "This is nice. Really nice. I watched everything, and I still don't know what you all put into it."

Argyle was smiling happily. "It is settling nicely. You have cooked for vampires before?"

Benny slurped. "Yes. For the given, not the taken."

He paused. "You really do have a complete education."

Tremble snorted. "You are just cluing into that now?"

Smith wasn't speaking, he was just slogging through his bowl as if afraid that the soup would disappear if he stopped touching it.

For Benny, it was a recipe that her great aunt had taught her on her seventeenth birthday. Since she wasn't really allowed to go out, it was a better idea to make her friends and family comfortable and happy. It was an old-fashioned idea, but her aunt was an old-fashioned woman. Three hundred years old and no relation to her at all.

Most of her relations were no relations. It was a fact of life that when you came from a line with this much power that you either spread your family wide or it boiled down to a single line. Each generation on either side had one child and that line culminated in Beneficia.

When Smith finished his meal, he picked up the dishes and washed them, putting them on the draining board with efficiency.

"So, Benny, what kind of shifters are in your bloodline?"

She sighed. "I only had two. My grandmother was a wolf shifter, and her father was a human multi-shifter."

"And some demon, a bit of human. How much fey?" Tremble smiled.

She shrugged. "They pop up now and then. Even some vampire makes itself known on my mother's side."

Argyle perked up. "Given or taken?"

"Given."

He looked relieved. "Do you know the sire?"

She chuckled. "Rumour is that she was a true given. No one knows for sure. She rarely returns for a visit."

Smith scowled. "What?"

Argyle looked at him. "Didn't you ever take vampire studies?"

Smith narrowed his eyes. "Pretend I didn't and refresh me."

"Two types of vampires. Those who come from a line that took immortality by violence and those who had it given to them. It is a very long and sad story, but that is the basis of it. I am a given vampire. I was offered this as a choice, and it does not come with the territory bindings or hierarchy that the taken vampires love."

Tremble sighed. "Smith knows; he just likes to make Argyle explain things. It is his personal form of entertainment."

Smith grinned. "It really is. These two constantly remind me that I am the youngest, so I make them over-explain things. It amuses me and irritates them, so we all win."

Benny chuckled and finished her soup. "If anyone needs to freshen up, there is a restroom down the hall and to the left. My parents will be occupied for another twenty minutes, so I think I will work on dessert."

Tremble arched his brow. "How do you know that it will take them twenty minutes?"

She looked at the clock. "It is time for them to have sex. My father's exposed nature increased his sex drive, so they have sex at regular intervals throughout the day, which allows him to keep his focus and continue his research."

Argyle blinked. "Sex?"

Benny pulled cupcakes out of the freezer and set them for a thaw cycle in the microwave. She fired up the coffee maker and got things underway. "Of course. My great grandmother was a succubus. The sex drive comes with the species.”

The three agents looked at each other nervously.

She snorted and pulled out ice cream and fruit. “You three shouldn’t look so shocked. There hasn’t been a shy and sheltered human in this house for the last twenty years.”

They looked at each other and Smith nodded. “Since your mother got ill.”

“Right. During her recovery and my father’s change, there was a house full of folk to protect me from my own parents as they adapted to their new status.” She peeled the paper cups off the cupcakes, set them in bowls and piled three different scoops of ice cream on each one before topping them with berries in sauce.

She slid the bowls in front of her guests and got the coffee. “It has been a long night, drink up.”

They sat in surprise and grabbed for the spoons she put in front of them. Her instincts for dessert had not abandoned her. She hoped to have hit every craving that the three had.

Smith paused and mumbled around his treat. "So, right now, your parents are having sex?"

"Yup. All the rooms are sound-proofed, but it is pretty much guaranteed with the stress of the last few days." She poked at her own cupcake.

Tremble arched his eyebrows. "Stress?"

He had a smear of blueberry on his cheek.

Benny grinned. "Yes, stress. It is hard enough for my parents to have me living outside their home without knowing that I would be exposed to danger. They have hidden me from the world, and suddenly, I was getting into a car with the same men who are duty-bound to throw me in custody for my bloodline the moment that my control slips."

She reached out and rubbed the blueberry off his cheek. She sucked the syrup off her thumb.

Argyle was staring at her, and Smith swallowed hard. She gathered their dishes and quickly washed everything. "Why are you guys boring a hole in my spine with your eyes?"

Tremble cleared his throat. "We have never arrested a demon blood before. I do not think that any of us put you in that category."

Benny kept washing and snorted. "You need to. It is what I am. With the mirror of my soul now off Jennifer, I am the last target. If I am attacked, my instincts will rise past my training and I will defend myself against the assault, no matter what you are doing."

When everything was on the draining board, she settled at the table and met their gazes, one by one. "So, which one of you likes to play with cuffs? I am pretty sure you are going to need them before this is over."

Lenora chuckled. "Benny, stop scaring them. None of them are used to aggression in females."

Her mother had a well-satisfied glow, and the agents suddenly didn't know where to look.

Her mother came up to her and kissed her forehead. "You told them."

Benny grinned. "Never be ashamed of what you are or how you were raised."

"Right. Well, your father is just about done on the sample. He has identified the classification of sponsoring demons, and with a little bit of help, you should be able to get a name."

The agents were on their feet in a heartbeat.

Lenora looked into the pot on the stove. "Noodles?"

"In the fridge."

"Thanks. I will make a tray for Harcourt. He has been worrying, and you know what that does for his appetites."

Benny nodded. "I know. I will distract him. The agents should do wonders."

Her mother's laughter rippled after them as they left the kitchen and headed for the lab.

"Your family seems peculiarly jovial given your circumstances." Tremble muttered.

"My mother and my father are bound for life, however long that is. The day that one dies, the other will pass so that neither will know the pain of living alone. I have grown up in that love as part of it. When they do pass, I may have preceded them or I may remain alone, but I will have the memory of their love around me. It is a pretty good feeling."

She pushed the door to the lab open, and she paused, "Arms in, gentlemen.

Don't touch anything. There are things in here I would not advise even the lightest of contacts with."

They all nodded, and she led the way to the active workspace. Her father was focussing on what appeared to be a PH strip with black boxes. He was measuring the tip of a glass rod covered with an inky substance.

His crest rose as he found his answer. "Son-of-a-two-headed-scum-sucking-bitch!"

Benny blinked. "Hiya, Dad. So, you found out what is doing this?"

He looked at her, and his pupils were completely black with fury. "I have to make a call."

He pushed past the agents, and Benny scrambled after him. "Dad? What is it?"

They converged in the library where her father was, indeed, making a call. The huge copper bowl filled with mercury swirled, and her grandfather's face was hovering above it.

"Where is she, father?"

Her grandfather, Zephyr Luciver Ganger, scowled. "What is it, son?"

"Kyria's father. He is after Benny."

Her grandfather had the urbane look of a studying magus. At four hundred eighty, he didn't look a day over fifty. His features were completely human if you didn't look at his slightly pointed ears and teeth, as well as the flickering shape of his pupils behind the reading glasses.

The mercury began to swirl. "After Benny? He cannot have her. She is not bound to him."

If Zephyr was getting agitated enough to effect the communication, his local weather must have been going haywire.

"Have you talked to your grandmother?" Zephyr's demon features were becoming more apparent as he got angry.

"No, if she is in the zone, they could track the call. I wanted to know if you have had recent communication with her. You are her son; you can speak without all the extra magework."

Her grandfather nodded. Benny waved from behind her dad. His expression softened for a moment before it hardened with determination. "I will get in touch with her and find out why Yomra is trying to come after Benny."

"It is worse than that, Dad. They are trying to strip her soul. There is a human agent who has been doing the work for him, but Yomra's signature is there for anyone to see."

"I trust your work, son. I will return your call within the hour or Kyria will. No one is touching Benny." Her grandfather disappeared.

The XIA agents looked at each other before Argyle asked, "Who is Yomra?"

Benny rubbed her forehead. "A whole new batch of trouble."

Chapter Twelve

They sat in the library. The agents called in, and Jennifer was stable, but there were no further leads on the case. What they learned here would show them their new direction.

Harcourt pulled up a chair, and they gathered around a book of demons. Benny flipped to her ancestor's page and she turned it around.

"Yomra. Demon high king, one of a dozen or so. He had dozens of children, but my great grandmother was supposedly his favourite."

The agents took in the etching of the demon king. Rich blue leathery skin, yellow eyes and spikes running down his spine made the biggest impression. The raging erection was also hard to miss.

"His deal was that he fathered children on human women for favours, and when they had born his heirs, he granted them their wishes until they passed on. Few, if any, survived childbirth. My great grandmother was one of those babies."

Benny picked up a book of succubi and flipped to her great grandmother's page. "Kyria worked for her father in demon tradition, carrying out the deals and seducing the weak-willed. My great grandfather traded some dark spell work for an heir by Kyria. Yomra agreed and was amused as hell. Succubi cannot breed with humans. Yomra had no clue as to how much Milton wanted to be with Kyria. He put all of his magic into their joining, and it produced my grandfather. Zephyr. The moment she was a mother, demon law broke her ties with

Yomra. Kyria was free, and Yomra was down one seducer. That was nearly five hundred years ago."

Her father nodded. "Benny is the first daughter born since then to our family line."

She turned Kyria's page to them, and she watched their gazes flick from her to the picture and back again. "I know. There is a resemblance."

Argyle nodded. "More than a resemblance. The eyes are the only difference."

Benny snorted. "I am four inches taller."

The house shook and the temperature spiked. "Only when you are wearing heels, kitten."

Benny grinned and ran to the other woman. "Gamma!"

Kyria held her and twirled her in her arms. "I hear that bad things are happening here."

It was like looking into a skewed mirror. Benny heard her mother sigh. "Hello, Kyria."

Her gamma looked over at Benny's mom. "Lenora. I see you have managed to hang onto my grandson."

Benny stepped away. "Mom and Dad are soul bonded, and it was his soul that did the bonding. Be nice, Gamma."

Kyria sighed and stroked Benny's cheek. "I like the eye. It looks good on you. You should be proud of what you are. Folks need to see it."

Benny sighed. "Gamma, these are XIA agents. Agent Smith, Agent Tremble and Agent Argyle. Agents, this is my great grandmother, Kyria Luciver."

The agents moved forward and shook her hand, one by one. Kyria's expression turned from amused to delight.

"Kitten, who knew you had so many men mooning after you. I confess that I am practically dizzy with admiration."

Kyria stroked their hands and forearms with focus.

Benny pinched the bridge of her nose. "They are not admirers. I am writing a piece for work. They volunteered to haul me around for a week. That is all."

Kyria shook her head, "Oh, kitten. You can be so blind when you want to be."

"I haven't been a kitten for ten years." Benny scowled.

"You will always be a kitten to me. Now, what do we think is going on here?"

Harcourt came over and greeted his grandmother with a kiss on the cheek. "I think someone is trying to hand Benny over to Yomra."

Kyria leaned back and hissed. "He has no claim over her. She is of his blood-line, but she has a soul."

It all snapped together in that mo-ment. Benny looked to her mother, and

Lenora nodded grimly. "The soul stripping spell."

"That one hasn't been used in eons." Kyria frowned.

Argyle nodded. "Until the last few months. Eight women across the country have had their souls and blood pulled out. They were all born the same week as Benny and in the same hospital."

Kyria nodded. "Right. The ninth?"

The agents homed in on that. Tremble asked, "How did you know there were nine?"

Kyria smiled. "Demons love numbers. If they didn't find what they needed in the first eight, they will need the ninth."

Benny nodded. "That is me now. Jennifer is out of the game. She is safe now."

Smith gave her a look. "That power surge..."

"Her soul is locked in her body now. There is no way that a separation can occur while she lives." She smirked. "Anyone who tries is going to blast their own consciousness twenty feet straight back."

"Way to go, kitten." Kyria chuckled and then sobered. "Now, Harcourt. Show me what you have found."

Benny stepped back and let the two demons in the room work on finding the third.

Argyle looked at her. "Should we be arresting someone?"

She chuckled. "Letter of the law is that a demon can only be arrested or detained while off their own territory or out of the demon zone and only then if they are found to be tampering with a human in an unseemly way. It does leave a lot of room for flexibility of the arresting officers."

Smith snorted. "You seem to be very aware of the laws."

She gave him a wry look. "What is the damage threshold before a shifter can be charged?"

"Four hundred thirty-four dollars."

Benny grinned. "It looks like you are very aware of the laws."

Colour tinted his cheeks. "Okay. Fair enough."

Argyle murmured. "What are they looking for?"

Lenora came over and whispered, "Kyria can locate her father, but I doubt he will actually be dumb enough to leave the zone. Kyria will be able to sense Yomra's energy and provide you with a tracking device."

Smith chuckled. "She doesn't appear to like you much, Mrs. Ganger."

Lenora laughed, "It has been fifty years since I stole her grandson into a life of academia and lust. The lust she could forgive, the life of study went beyond the pale. She dreamed of a life of success in the public eye for her grandson. With me, he glowed in the shadows."

Benny turned to her mother and beckoned for a moment. They crossed the room and bent their heads together in the hallway.

"What did Gamma mean about the agents and me?"

Lenora chuckled and hugged her. "Don't worry about it. These things reveal themselves in time. Demons live in the moment and pursue them, but you are more than that. Let your moments come to you."

Benny read the truth in her mother's eyes. There was something on the side of the agents, but she didn't know which ones. "Do I have to pick one?"

Lenora laughed. "Baby, in this family, you have the right to choose whatever blend of love makes you happy. Don't force it to be one-size-fits-all."

Benny hugged her mom and felt better about the diagnosis. She liked the agents and having seen one of them completely naked and a pretty good idea about the other two, the idea of trying them on for size held a certain appeal.

She returned to the library to find Kyria between Smith and Argyle, rubbing their arms.

"Gamma! Hands off."

Kyria sighed and released the men. They turned to Benny with dazed expressions.

She sighed and pulled them away from her seductive grandmother. A light tap on the cheek was enough to bring each one around. Tremble was wisely giving Kyria a wide berth.

Benny's father finally announced. "Grandmother, please put the tracking charm into place. They need to find this man."

"It is already dawn. They cannot use the charm until the evening." She cast the enchantment anyway.

Benny perked up. "Oh, they are off duty now."

Harcourt put the charm in a box and handed it to Tremble. "Here you go. This will take you directly to the man with Yomra's energy. It has been dulled to our family, so that should not cause interference."

Tremble took it.

Benny noted that even the ageless fey looked exhausted. "Why don't you guys go to bed? You can drop me at my house, and Jessamine is more than enough to warn me of any incoming weirdness."

Smith raised his hand. "I will stay at your home. You are the last option for a victim, and Argyle sleeps too heavily to be a good guardian."

Benny nodded. "Right. Well, it was great seeing you, Gamma."

She hugged her grandmother, gave her dad a hug and kissed and hugged her mother before heading out the door with the XIA.

Quiet exhaustion reigned in the vehicle as Argyle drove back to her place. Smith and Benny got out with Smith pausing for a moment to get some kind of order from the other two.

Benny headed inside. "Jess, we have company."

Jessamine floated in, and she wrinkled her spectral forehead. "Really?"

"Yes. One of the Agents is staying with me over the course of the day. I am being hunted."

Jess nodded. "I will make something for when you wake. Water is already in your room, and the moment you lie down, I will dim the lights."

"Thanks, Jess."

Smith came in with a small bag. "So, where are we sleeping?"

Jess floated toward him. "Benny's is the only room with a bed, so you will have to share."

Benny gave her a dark look. It would only take seconds to make up one of the guestrooms.

Smith nodded. "Right. Meet you there."

He headed past her and up the stairs.

Benny glared at her intangible roommate and swatted her furiously. "Really? Really?"

"He's cute. Besides, he is still on duty. Nothing is going to happen. You need to relax and let folks enjoy you for the multifaceted being that you are, Benny."

Benny suddenly felt her exhaustion, every moment of being awake, the running, the accidents, every instance of the last two days. "Can you have my owl jammies meet me in the bathroom?"

"Will do. Go on. I will watch over you."

She headed upstairs with her limbs collecting lead with every step. Smith had removed his shirt, and the sight perked her up enough to head directly into the bathroom. She got ready for bed and put on her owl jammies before she stumbled out into the bedroom.

He was wearing boxer briefs and nothing else. "What side do you sleep on?"

She yawned. "Right side. Closest to the bathroom."

He nodded and grinned. "Nice pajamas."

She blushed a little and climbed into bed. Smith did the same on the left side, and she felt a moment of concern. That moment faded as the room darkened and her body felt its fatigue. Using magic to avoid sleep resulted in a coma-like event. With Smith and Jessamine on duty, she was as safe as she could be.

Benny snuggled under her sheets and muttered, "Jess, get us up one hour before sundown."

A cool hand smoothed her hair, and she heard, "Rest, kitten. I will keep you safe."

Benny tried to fight the wave of sleep when she heard Kyria's voice, but she was too tired. Darkness pulled in tight around her.

Chapter Thirteen

Harcourt watched as his grandmother reappeared. Kyria smiled. "She is safe."

He exhaled and took his wife's hand, pressing a kiss to the back of it. "The wards are in place?"

"He would have to be driving a tank to get through them." Kyria smiled. "I used the vial Lenora gave me. The house is guarded by nature. No demon magic is visible."

Harcourt smiled. "Good. Yomra is arrogant. He will be expecting us to fight magic to magic. Benny has so much more to battle with, and if she lets herself, she is able to use all of it."

He looked to his wife and saw her worry. "She will come out of this alive, Lenora."

She stroked his head and neck in an absent way. "I know she will, Harcourt, but I believe that other things are going to rise."

"You mean..."

"Yes." She glanced at the Kyria and didn't say anything else.

Kyria poured tea for them and smiled. "You mean when the little bastard who tried to rape Benny mysteriously died from having his soul inverted? It was the last demon attack in this town and the only one for a hundred years before that. It got attention."

Harcourt smiled grimly. "He had assaulted four other girls, but Benny got away with a broken wrist and some scratches. She didn't want to return to school with him there, so I managed the situation."

Kyria smirked. "And you did as any good father would do if he had the skills."

Lenora was quiet. Harcourt kissed the back of her hand again. The killing haunted her for reasons Kyria did not need to know.

"I would do it again. He was a rabid parasite, living on the pain he inflicted." Harcourt nodded. "Now, what do we do about finding your father?"

Kyria shrugged. "I have carried out what I could. The rest is up to you. He is bound by demon laws to stay away from me. I will watch to see what happens, but I have offered all the help I can. The rest is up to you and those born free from the touch of the zone."

Harcourt was astonished when his grandmother disappeared.

Lenora sighed. "I thought she would pull that move. Speak to Zephyr and bring him up to date. Perhaps your mother would have an opinion of the matter."

He chuckled. "She is very opinionated for one in her situation."

"Gender equality began long after she died. She is looking forward to learning and seeing Benny do more with her life than Lettice ever dreamed of."

He wrinkled his nose. His mother had already passed on when Benny was born, but that had not stopped her from being involved in her granddaughter's life.

"Right. I'll speak to my mother. She will have some insight into this matter."

Harcourt went to the desk, and he pulled out a glossy brown case. Inside the carefully crafted case was a velvet bag, and inside the bag was a medallion with two of his mother's fangs and one of her claws from when she shifted. She had donated the implements when she had begun her decline, and Zephyr had woven them into the medallion as a gift for his son.

Harcourt held the medallion in his hand and smiled. "Mother?"

Lettice Ganger flowed out of the medallion and stood next to her son. "Harcourt. It is so good to see you again. You have grown."

He chuckled. "I have not."

Lenora smiled. "Good morning, Lettice."

Lettice beamed, "Lenora. You are looking well. Where is little Benny?"

Lenora chuckled. "Little Benny is thirty years old, and she is in danger."

Harcourt watched his mother glide across the floor and sit in a chair, her Edwardian clothing as precise as it always had been.

"Explain what is going on, and I will tell you what my opinion is on the matter." Lettice drummed her spectral fingers on the table and waited.

Harcourt and Lenora sat with her and explained the situation. After an hour, Lettice made her comment.

"This isn't good. Benny is going to have to run this out, but this isn't good. Lenora, call your family and have them on standby. If anything goes sideways, we are going to need to hide her and do it quickly. An untethered demon is a danger to society, and they know it." Lettice frowned. "Damn, I wish I could have a cup of tea."

Harcourt watched as Lenora focussed on her palm, and she wove a cup of tea out of ectoplasm.

With a smile, Lenora handed the tea to her mother-in-law.

Lettice beamed and sipped at the cup. "Oh, that is lovely. You learned that spell for me?"

Lenora smiled. "I have been holding onto it just in case."

"Now, can you do the same trick with a nice rare steak?"

Lenora laughed. "I can, but it will take about an hour."

"Well, I am a shifter and not a magic user, but life with Zephyr taught me a lot. If Benny has you backing her and family ready to gather around her, she can survive this."

Lenora scowled. "What do you mean? I am sure she will weather the assassin."

Lettice waved that away. "I am speaking of the public exposure of her family and bloodlines. There is no avoiding that now. She will be exposed as a blend of species that no one thought could even breed. She will go from being sheltered to a publicly acknowledged freak. That is why she will need family and friends. Her life is about to shift, and it will never be the same, no matter the outcome."

Harcourt let his mother's words sink in, and he nodded. "Lenora, get on the phone. We need to be ready."

He glanced at his wife and smiled, she was already on the phone, and she was making a list with her free hand. Lenora's grasp of modern technology was one of the things he loved about her, one of the things out of thousands. He could not imagine life without her and Benny in it, and it was that love that kept him in touch with the part of him that was born human.

Having a man wrapped around her was definitely a novel way to wake up. Benny tried to ease free of Smith's body, but he tightened his arms the moment she moved.

She had to pee.

She sighed and pried his arms away, slipping out from under the covers and making her way to the bathroom. After she relieved herself, she washed her hands, scrubbed her face and brushed her teeth again. As she crept into the bedroom, she checked the time, and it was only just turning eleven. She still had four hours to sleep at the minimum.

Benny flipped back the covers, and Smith had taken up the available space. She huffed. With a determined focus, she rolled him to his other side and scooted into the bed, bracing her back against his.

She felt him trembling slightly, and she turned her head as she tucked herself in. "Are you laughing, Smith?"

"Maybe. I did not expect you to flip me over." He got out of bed and headed for the bathroom.

She chuckled and wormed her way back under the bedding, pulling the covers up and over her ears. When he returned, he wrapped his arms around her again, and he made a happy grunt when he pulled her against him.

"This is a little odd considering that as far as I know your first name is Agent."

He chuckled and sighed against her neck. "William. My first name is William. Argyle's is James, and Tremble's name is Hurias."

She smiled. "Nice to meet you, William. Hands stay in neutral territory."

He sighed. "You are no fun."

"Fun comes after stopping the guy trying to psychically rip me to pieces. For now, I will settle for a bit more sleep." She squirmed against him for a moment before she settled in to sleep.

Her squirming had made sure that his sleep was a little further away than hers, but that was what he got for hogging the bed.

The scent of breakfast for dinner got Benny out of bed a few hours later. She got dressed and tiptoed down the stairs.

"Jessamine?" The whisper shouldn't carry, but while Benny could smell food, she couldn't hear any of the noises that she associated with breakfast.

She stood in the kitchen and called out, "Jess?"

There was no answer and that was unusual. Jess was always available even if she was doing double duty down at the main house.

She looked around, but it was when she spotted the portrait of her and her parents that she knew something had gone wrong. Her father was his dapper green self and that was not the portrait in her home, it was the one in her mind.

Benny ran upstairs, and she tried to wake Smith, but he was still wrapped around her. She had been disembodied.

Snarling, Benny jumped on top of her body, and she thrashed around. Smith snorted and Benny looked at him with narrowed eyes. She slowly and carefully eased into him, hiding inside his larger form. His aura shuddered as she made room for herself, but when the shadows crept up the stairs, she was glad that she had hidden.

Gremlins crawled along the walls, chittering to themselves as they sought her out. She had been pulled into the space between worlds. When the gremlins ran their hands through her body and came up empty, the chittering took on a panicked tone.

She watched as they avoided touching Smith, and when he moved, she rolled with him. Keeping inside him was paramount.

The gremlins searched every inch of her bedroom before they started to crackle and explode, one by one.

She counted down from the dozen she had witnessed until the twelfth gremlin exploded. It was not the right number. Demons didn't use even numbers.

Three minutes passed until the final gremlin crept from beneath the bed. He was larger than the rest and looked like he had accumulated the bodies of his fallen brethren.

The aura she was nestled in snapped tight around her. It was in defense rather than attack so she held still.

The gremlin looked at her body, and he ran his hand down her cheek, over her breasts in a lewd gesture.

Smith's aura sat up, and he flexed his claws. He slashed at the gremlin, and the beast staggered back. The roar that Smith let out caused the gremlin's entire body to ripple. They locked together in combat, and Benny was along for the ride.

They slashed, hacked and clawed at each other on the psychic plane. Benny could feel the protective anger that Smith was channelling, and it drove him forward until their attacker was carved into strips by the lion's claws.

When the gremlin was gone, the room itself lightened.

Benny's body stirred and sat up, and just like that, she was pulled out of Smith and back where she belonged.

She sat up, still in her pajamas. She prodded Smith in the shoulder, and he shot out of bed.

His half-shift was impressive, but his tail had to be uncomfortable in those shorts.

"What the hell was that?"

Benny rubbed her forehead and felt a trace of oil that was more than natural. "Soul separation. Kyria came to me as I was falling asleep, and I felt her touch my forehead. I need a shower."

"Is it safe?"

"To take a shower? Yes. To keep the mark on my skin? No."

She headed into the bathroom and started the water. Her clothing went flying, and she turned to step into the shower when she realised that she had left the door open and Smith was an interested audience.

She kicked the door mostly closed and stepped under the spray, soaping up and scrubbing her forehead. Gamma had some explaining to do.

Chapter Fourteen

They entered the main house, and Benny flicked one of the portraits on the wall. The lockdown was immediate.

Kyria was sitting with her grandson, and she paled when Benny entered the room.

"Why, Gamma, you look surprised to see me."

The obvious attempt to teleport stretched space around the succubus.

Harcourt got to his feet, glaring at his grandmother. "What did you do?"

Kyria looked around with wild eyes and tried to find an exit.

Lenora muttered quickly, and bands of power wrapped around her grandmother-in-law.

Kyria was suspended in midair and unable to do anything. Every bit of her was confined, Lenora made sure of it.

Benny explained the sleep visit to her father and mother. Her father's crest came up, and her mother seethed. "It is fine. Thanks to Agent Smith, I am perfectly fine."

She walked up to her genetic twin and asked, "I just don't know why."

Kyria tried to speak, but Lenora had her all wrapped up.

Benny threw a translation orb into the air.

I want another child, but my mate is a demon. He is also beholden to Yomra, and if we have a child, I will be back where I started five centuries ago. I want another child, so Yomra offered a compromise. I could provide another female born of my flesh to take my place.

You are the only daughter of my blood, kitten. Kyria's eyes begged for understanding.

Benny tightened her fist and the orb shattered. "Don't call me kitten."

Smith put his hands on her shoulders. "Easy, Benny. It is over."

She turned to look at him with astonishment. "It isn't her that has been killing across the country. Yomra took her suggestion and decided to go around her. If he can get two females of his bloodline to do his will, he would increase his power exponentially. He convinced a gullible human to do his work for him, and they have been following the power lines until it led to me."

"If they knew where you were, why didn't they come here?"

She closed her eyes. "They were leaving me with nowhere to run."

"So, before, you could have put your mind into anyone of those bodies?" Smith's fingers were tight on her shoulders.

"Yes, but only if this one was coopted. It explains the blood portion of the ritual. They are destroying the bodies so I can't use them."

Smith nodded. "Right, so this is more than personal, this is high demonology."

Lenora flicked her fingers and Grandma Lettice appeared.

Benny smiled. "Grandma!"

Lettice floated over and wrapped her arms around Benny. "I am so sorry that Kyria is such a selfish bitch, but she is a demoness and that must be remembered."

"I know. It is why she was the first one that I suspected. Dad's altered portrait was my big clue. He was more demony than even I could imagine. It is how she sees him, or how she wants to see him."

A knock at the door got Benny's attention. "I will get it. Keep the bindings up."

Tremble and Argyle were at the door. Argyle was wearing a heavy set of shades and his hood was up, but he looked rested.

Benny grabbed them and pulled them through the ward before resetting it again. "There have been developments."

"Where is the amulet?"

Argyle frowned. "I left it in the car."

She sighed. "Thank goodness."

"Why?"

"I am pretty sure that Kyria spiked it."

She beckoned them inside. "We will explain."

They gathered in the library, and everyone was brought up to speed.

Benny smiled at the agents. "You get to see why it is so seldom that folks arrest demons."

Smith growled. "She attacked you."

"Did she? She manipulated a member of her family and used gremlins to investigate the world between in search of me. To anyone from the outside, it would look like she was concerned."

Smith opened and closed his mouth. "Can't we get her for targeting you and removing you from your body?"

"Why? I am fine now. If you hadn't been holding me as we slept, you would never have known what happened."

Tremble and Argyle glared at Smith. Benny saw her parents give her amused glances, and Lettice stared at the three agents before smiling.

"Oh, gentlemen, this is my grand-mother, Lettice."

Lettice smiled. "I am pleased to meet you. I have been working with Harcourt and Lenora to create a more reliable tracking device. I have designed something that should work."

Kyria tried to squirm free of her bonds, but Lenora tightened the restraints.

Benny kept glancing at her great grandmother. She was about to demon out, and it was something that the agents needed to see.

Lettice and Harcourt went to the workbench, and Benny joined them.

A few drops of the soil sample, some oil of rabbit's foot, a dash of snake venom for focus and finding the path, a drop of Benny's blood to bring it all together and enough magic to hold it around a crystal. The luck was an extra touch that Benny added. She felt she could use it.

Benny held up the new charm and nodded. "Perfect. I just have to go to the lab to get something."

She wound the chain around her fingers and smiled brightly. Kyria got to her frustration mark, and the agents backed away. Vivid purple-scaled skin, three head waves, black on black eyes and a set of fangs that didn't look like blow jobs should be on the menu.

She waved her hand from the agents to the very angry demoness near the ceiling. "And that is why you don't cast a demon sex spell. That is what lies beneath."

They stood with their eyes wide, and she went to the lab to get the aerosol nullifier as well as a vial of liquid. She tucked the liquid container into her cleavage and held the spray in the hand opposite her new tracking charm.

She returned to the library and hugged her parents. "This should be enough to settle things tonight."

Her father held her tight. "Take care, and if anything happens, come home immediately. We will take care of you."

Her mother whispered, "What your father said. You can always come home, Beneficia."

Benny nodded and headed to the door. "Keep an eye on Kyria. She might try to run when we break the warding."

Harcourt nodded. "We will be watching her."

The agents followed her to the car, and she smiled at Argyle. "Can you bring the other charm out?"

He nodded and reached into the car, careful not to touch the surface of the metal. He looked at her. "Now what?"

She kicked over a stone edging the drive and smoothed it clean with her foot. She sprayed the neutraliser on the rock and nodded. "Put it down there."

He set it down on the rock, and a sizzle came from the charm. When he stepped back, she worked the spray over the charm from the bottom to the top, including the chain. It sizzled and crackled as the coating magic covered and blanked out the demon magic.

The charm burst into flame, and it confirmed that there wasn't simply benign tracking magic involved.

Never trust a charm you don't make yourself. Her mother had chanted it over and over. Benny never imagined that she wouldn't be able to trust family.

With the new charm in her fist, she looked at the agents. "Do you want to call for backup?"

They looked at each other and shook their heads. Smith added, "Not unless we can't handle what happens. We don't want you exposed or endangered."

She quirked her lips. "Gentlemen, the moment that we get a heading, I will want all the backup you can call. My life is immaterial, catching the man who would make a deal with a demon by killing eight women and attempting to kill a ninth, all for some power we don't know about, is paramount."

Benny opened her door in the SUV and looked at them. "What if the demon in question shows up?"

Argyle got behind the wheel, Smith at the computer and Tremble was in the back with her once again. Benny put the neutraliser spray down with the safety on and switched the charm to her right hand. From her seat, she leaned forward and sent power through the chain. The charm lifted and swung back toward the main road.

Argyle nodded and said, "Tremble, you keep on the directions. Watch the charm and tell me which way to go. Benny, stay buckled in and keep behind me."

She chuckled. "To think, only a few days ago, we were after psychic hookers selling magical seduction, and today, we are trying to stop someone working for one of my relatives from ripping my guts out. Ah, evolution."

Tremble raised his brows and chuckled. "I thought that I had problems with my family."

Benny sighed. "The more races you add, the more possibilities for problems. This is just one part of my bloodline. The rest can be better or worse depending on where you are standing."

Argyle smiled at her in the rear-view mirror. "That sounds like a series of stories."

Night embraced the interior of the car, and Tremble's low voice droned the directions.

"It is quite entertaining. Some species shouldn't be in the same room together." She chuckled.

They continued on their way until Tremble asked, "What does it mean when it is twirling?"

"We are here."

They were next to a cemetery, and it was obvious where they needed to go.

Once outside the car, each of the agents got a weapon from the back of the vehicle. This was serious. They were not going in alone.

"Call for backup." Benny insisted.

Smith sighed and reported that hostile figures had been sighted in the cemetery along with stray magic. Backup was nine minutes away.

Benny nodded. "Right. Now, we can do this."

She lifted the charm, and it lifted straightforward, leading them to the gates. "Now or never."

Tremble flicked two long butterfly knives open. "I vote never."

Smith clenched his fists around the studded and bladed grips that covered his hands. "Voting never as well."

Argyle shrugged. "I vote now so that Benny can get on with her life."

Benny grinned. "And I vote now, and I get two votes because I am a woman."

Smith looked like he wanted to argue, but Tremble put his hand on the lion's shoulder. "Don't contradict her."

Snickering, Benny led the way.

The rich smell of loam mixed with the green scent of oaks and the tang of pine. There were no fresh graves in the cemetery, which was very odd given the amount of empty spaces available.

Benny watched as the crystal lead them right into one of those vacant expanses.

She held her hand up and the other three paused. "Something's wrong."

She put more power into the crystal, and shadows began to shift in the open space. The shadows collected and coalesced into a single figure. It was the man who had taken Jennifer.

"Finally, you have come to me." He smiled, and it was not a good smile.

She could see the twenty-foot circle around him.

Benny quickly extended her arms to either side. "Bite me."

The dark figure laughed, but Argyle and Smith followed her orders. She winced as the teeth went in and each man took in her blood. She turned her head to Tremble and whispered, "Kiss me."

He took in the hint and threaded his fingers through her hair, pulling her head back and kissing her.

She exhaled her power, and Tremble's kiss became possessive. As Argyle and

Smith released her, she had to press her hands to the elf's to get him to let her go.

When Tremble staggered back, his eyes were glowing. Argyle and Smith were doing the same.

Benny chuckled. "Now, gentlemen. Please come with me."

The shadow man had watched with amusement, but when all four of them passed the edge of his circle, he freaked.

"Not possible! Only demon energy can pass that circle." He brandished a rod, and it glowed bright.

She recognised the symbol branded into the first woman and Jennifer.

She didn't bother explaining blood and power transfers. He didn't need to know.

He lunged at her, and Tremble moved between them. When the man raised his rod and attacked, the elf nimbly danced to one side, bringing both blades down into the back of the shadow's wrist.

The scream shook the trees. The branding rod rolled across the grass. The agents surrounded the shadow and went after him, pummelling and slashing at him. Benny went for the branding iron.

She tore off her sleeve and wrapped it around the handle. She didn't want to touch it if she didn't have to.

The shadow was still fighting, but it was slowing.

"Can you hold his head?"

They shifted, and she moved behind the shadow man, pressing the glowing glyph to the back of his head. He screamed and began to float. Well, he tried to float. The agents still had control of him.

Benny whispered, "Let him go. I have marked him with his owner's sign. He is about to be reclaimed."

The agents stumbled back just as backup arrived. The man soared up, and shadows emerged from around him, taking his body apart inch by inch.

Benny pulled out the nullifier from between her breasts, and she poured it over the branding iron from the still-smouldering head to the handle. She coated it and watched it writhe and twist on the ground as the enchantment that it held crumbled to dust.

She staggered out of the circle with the agents and collapsed on the ground.

A vampire XIA agent walked up to her and said, "Beneficia Ganger?"

She nodded. She knew what was coming. "I am."

"You are under arrest for twisting the loyalties of the XIA agents assigned to your ride-along."

She held out her wrists, and the cuffs went on. At least she could get some sleep in a nice safe cell. "Take me away."

Chapter Fifteen

$\mathcal{B}$enny sat in processing while they tried to cleanse Smith, Argyle and Tremble of her influence.

She was fingerprinted, had ocular scans run and had to provide a blood sample. "This is a little involved, isn't it?"

The woman doing the processing sneered. "Demon spawn need to be watched at all times. We need to know what you are and where you are at every moment of the day so that you won't spread your influence."

Benny sighed. "Of course not."

"Why did you physically contaminate the agents?"

"So that they could make it through the protective circle this time. The first time we tracked the killer, they were blocked by the spell."

"How was it that you were able to make it through?" Officer Rorik sneered at her.

"It was keyed for demon frequencies."

"How did you know that?"

Benny snorted. "I didn't. I thought that the agents would get there before I did. I am not a hero."

"Of course you aren't."

Benny pinched the bridge of her nose. "I am a journalist, and I write recipes for a blog. That is it. I don't have any weapons or attack training. I don't know what to do when someone takes a swing at me. I avoid confrontation at all costs."

"So, how did someone as cowardly as you come to be ripping apart a demon's avatar?"

Benny blinked. "Is that what that was? I thought it was a seduced soul being used. It was an actual projection?"

"Answer the question."

"I simply did to the shadow man what he did to the victims. I thought it would create a hole by which the soul would be pulled to the one yanking on his strings."

"Because you thought that it was a projected soul and not the actual demon."

"Correct." Benny lifted both hands and drank some truly horrible coffee. Her cuffs clanked as she moved.

"Why didn't you resist arrest?"

"I knew you were coming. Sort of. I knew that one way or another, the demons would move to put me in custody."

Officer Rorik stared at her with wide eyes. "What?"

"Out of the last nine generations, I am only one part human, two parts demon and the rest is something else. The demons are pernicious, but they are part of me. I can't do anything about that, but I can keep that part of me under control. Every. Day. Of. My. Life."

The officer was staring at her, mouth open.

Benny flexed her wrists but didn't try to release herself.

The officer got to her feet. "Just a moment."

Benny waited with her senses banked and her mind quiet. The agents would be fine the moment that her blood left their systems after a good meal. Tremble just had to exhale near a tree and he would be clear. She hadn't harmed anyone and there wasn't really anything to charge her with other than unlawful seduction. The last time she checked, seducing a man without sleeping with him wasn't a crime if she didn't use magic. It wasn't even a crime if she did use magic. This was racism pure and simple.

After twenty minutes of quiet, the door opened and Captain Matheson and the XIA attorney, Ms. Wingart, came through the open doorway.

"Ms. Ganger, can you please come with us?" The captain was serious.

She lifted her hands and the chains clanged. "I would love to, but I need a little help."

Ms. Wingart turned to the officer. "Chains off. Now."

Officer Rorik paused, "But she is a demon."

"Chains. Now."

The officer walked over and slowly unlocked the cuffs. She was glaring at Benny the entire time.

Benny rubbed her wrists and got to her feet. She knew she was hardly intimidating, but the woman flinched away.

Benny looked at the captain. "Be honest. It is the eye, isn't it?"

The captain chuckled. "Of course. Please come with us. We have a proposal for you."

The lawyer took her by the arm and walked out with her as friendly as could be. She was escorted out of the Magic Enforcement Unit and down the underground tunnel to the XIA.

Ms. Wingart said, "You have to pardon the ME Unit. They suffer from a lack of imagination and even less humour."

"I am aware of it. I didn't want to undo the cuffs and break her sense of security, but their spell work is exceptionally sloppy."

The lawyer laughed. "I know. I think they like to attack our kind when they run. I have no idea why you were there to begin with."

Benny shrugged. "I am not a shifter and I look human. I was exhausted after a very trying few days."

Captain Matheson smiled. "I have read the reports. Despite what the ME Unit would have you believe, our agents were keeping us informed of their growing attachment to you. I have spoken with your parents, and the spectrum of attraction has now been explained to my satisfaction."

The lawyer cleared her throat. "We will continue this discussion in our offices."

The rest of their walk was silent. When they got to the scanner, Benny walked through it without any trouble. Her demon side was well and truly tamped down.

The captain raised his eyebrows, but didn't say a word until they got to his office.

He held a chair for her, and she dropped into the comfortable leather with a groan. Ms. Wingart got her some water and a pastry from a sideboard and put them on the desk within easy reach.

"Smith, Tremble and Argyle have been given clean bills of health on all scores. They are still infatuated by you and that brings me to the reason you are here."

Benny leaned back with the pastry cradled in her palms. "What?"

"I want you to take agent training and join their team as a magical specialist. The agents speak highly of your skills with spell casting and your ability to think on your feet."

She nodded and worked through the Danish. "Wha abou duh demong fing?"

Ms. Wingart chuckled. "For the days when you slip up, we will get you a special pass. We think you would be a valued member of our team, and we are willing to back you in whatever court proceedings are going to shake loose from this."

Benny knew what she meant. "Jennifer."

"Correct. There is no suit pending, but there is the potential for one. It all depends on her."

Benny blinked. "I would like to speak with her. I have to explain what happened to her."

"That is not advisable."

She finished her pastry and grabbed for the water. "If I had been cursed my entire life, and then, it had been lifted, leaving me floating around with no clue as to what I really was, I would really like to know it."

The captain nodded. "We will investigate her state of mind. If she is considered stable, you will be allowed to meet with her with legal representation present."

Benny yawned. "Can I think about the offer?"

Ms. Wingart nodded, but she produced a simple contract. "Here is the offer to train you as an agent with a probationary period of six months beginning after your two weeks of protocol briefing."

Benny scanned the contract and blinked. "There is a provision in here allowing me to date members of my team in direct contradiction of the standard agent regulations."

Ms. Wingart nodded, and her head shifted into that of an eagle before returning to human. "We thought it would ease tensions if you could act on your impulses."

She had a brief image of the agents naked and quickly shook her head. "I do not feel that it is a good idea."

Ms. Wingart smiled and got her briefcase. "Fine. Stroke out the clause."

She left the room, and Benny and the captain were on their own.

Captain Matheson smiled. "If I were in Smith's pride, I would have ordered him to court you. I am not. If I were in Tremble's clan, I would have ordered the same. In Argyle's case, I would have talked to Mathias and gotten him to tell Argyle to take his head out of his ass. The problem lies in that I can't encourage one without encouraging all three. It would be bad for morale."

Benny blinked. "All three? I am supposed to take all three?"

Matheson blushed. "Not at the same time, but I believe that each of them offers you something unique. Two can even act as your mate if you want to start a family. I normally don't butt into the affairs of my people, but this is an exceptional situation and you are all exceptional beings."

Benny held up her hand. "Spare me. My ancestors have been down this road before. I don't have lions in my bloodline, so Smith is viable. All of my fey ancestors are powerful, but lower grade, so a high-grade fey is desirable. This is a conversation my family has been throwing my way for a decade. Are we related?"

He chuckled. "No, but I know your aunt, Reedana. She is a persuasive woman."

Her aunt Reedana was more siren than woman, but she did have a powerful way of speaking. If she wanted something, she could argue until you simply surrendered. The woman had stamina.

"Are you dating her?"

He laughed. "I am not that stupid. She is a friend of my wife's."

Benny chuckled, and she continued looking over the contract. Aside from the free rein to date her coworkers, there was nothing objectionable in the document.

She looked up at the captain and debated her options. In the end, there was only one.

"Can I have a pen?"

He handed it over to her with a flourish. When she signed her name, he did the same and grinned. "Welcome to the team, Agent-in-Training Ganger."

Benny smiled. "It sounds weird, but I have been called worse."

"That's the spirit. Now, let's get you a uniform." He rose to his feet and offered her his hand when he was next to her.

With a sense of finality, she put her hand in his and let him guide her through the halls and down to get an ID badge created with a demon-scan override. It was a solid start.

Chapter Sixteen

With her ID, uniform, bag and orientation textbooks, Benny stumbled into the parking lot outside XIA headquarters.

Pooky was waiting for her with his motor running. Freddy was in the passenger's seat.

Benny put her stuff in the trunk, and Pooky opened the driver's door for her. Grinning at her friend, she first greeted the car. "Thanks for the lift, Pooky."

Freddy was trying to look perturbed and failing miserably. "Well, since you won't come to the mountain, my wonderful self came to you."

"Hiya, Freddy. I would hug you, but Pooky is trying to look like a car." She reached out and squeezed her friend's hand.

"So, you have had a helluva week."

Benny began to giggle and then howl at the understatement. "I am nearly done with the article for Julian. It should be ready to upload in about an hour."

"He will be delighted, but he really wants to ask you to write a column about XIA training."

"Sorry. I just signed a confidentiality agreement."

Freddy laughed. "Damn."

"I can hear your disappointment."

Pooky drove them safely and sedately back to the Ganger house. Benny just enjoyed hanging onto her friend as a solid link to normality.

It was funny what a few days with the XIA made her think of as normal.

Her homecoming was warm, full of friends, food and drink. Her mother had called in all of her relatives, and they were there to greet Benny when she returned from her adventures.

When Benny got her parents alone, she asked softly. "So what did you do with her?"

Lenora smiled. "We mailed her back home. She will have to explain her failure to her father and her proposed mate. We can only hope they were not one and the same."

Benny shuddered, and her father squeezed her shoulders. "Bleah."

"I have felt a greatly reduced pressure on my own demonic tendencies, so I believe she has been trying to urge me into some sort of action in order to endanger you." Harcourt was solemn.

Benny nodded. "It is possible. I know that you two are going to have difficulty dealing with my news."

Lenora smiled. "What news?"

"I have been invited to train as an agent with the XIA. I have accepted."

The hands on her shoulders tightened, but then relaxed. "It is the right thing for you, Benny. Even I can sense it, and I have little to no empathy."

Lenora chuckled. "I am pleased for you. It is the first decision you have made for yourself to propel your skills forward. I am just surprised it took this long."

She shared a moment with her parents before the cheerful chatter of the party went quiet.

Benny looked toward the door where the three agents were standing with nervous determination. She went forward to make the introductions, but Freddy got there before her.

"Everybody, these are Benny's XIA agents. She will be working with them. Be nice."

Benny grinned and made the introduction that mattered. "Smith, Argyle and Tremble, this is Freddy. Freddy and I have been friends since we were children."

Freddy preened. "Play your cards right and I know all her secrets. I am amenable to bribery."

Argyle smiled, Smith chuckled and Tremble kissed Freddy's hand.

The tension was broken, and the party returned to its happy chatter.

Smith looked around the room, and he whistled softly. "I recognise a lot of the faces here. Is that a dragon?"

Benny smiled and hauled them through the party and out onto the balcony. She pulled up an aura of silence around them and sighed. "Thank you for coming, but why are you here?"

Smith chuckled. "Well, after the day we spent in bed together..."

She gave him a droll look. "Oh, shut up. Now, there are a lot of people inside that you will recognise from television and movies, as well as activists and academics. Be nice and remember you are not on duty. That said, thank you for coming."

She went up on her toes and kissed Smith softly. Benny stepped away and kissed Tremble, sliding her hand up behind his head and pulling him down to her. Tremble held her gently as if he was afraid he would spook her.

She smiled at him as she drew back.

Argyle didn't wait. The moment she turned to him, he wrapped his arms around her, dipped her and pressed his lips to hers.

Benny caught a glimpse of the crowd staring at them through the windows.

Freddy flared up and shooed them away, shot her a thumbs-up and kept guard.

Argyle's skin was cool, but it warmed rapidly where she touched him. When he set her back on her feet, her senses were spinning.

"Wow. Um, okay. I was just welcoming you to the gathering, but that took it to a whole new level." She patted her hair and the agents were laughing at her.

Smith smiled. "Well, now that we have been officially welcomed, I saw a delightful buffet inside and I really want to meet that dragon."

Benny patted his arm. "Stay away from Zora. Regick is really protective of her right now."

Argyle looked toward the room. "I saw a gargoyle in there, and I have always wanted to meet one."

Tremble straightened his shoulders and looked toward the gathering. "There are some high-court fey in there."

Benny laughed. "Go. Socialise. Have fun. Try and find out which guests are toxic and which are not."

Smith slid his arm around her waist, Argyle took the other side and Tremble put his hand on the vampire's shoulder. They returned to the party en masse, and the joy wrapped around them and pulled them in.

The ghosts sat out on a spectral balcony and had their own party.

Lettice poured for Jessamine and smiled. "I am so proud of how Benny has come through this."

Jess nodded at the other ghost. "It isn't over, but she has done well so far."

Lettice smirked. "Even dead, you seers can suck all the fun out of life."

Jess laughed. "I had to pull a lot of strings to get my remains assigned to the Ganger household. The mages didn't want to let me that close to this kind of power."

Lettice chuckled. "You are handling it well, and we have more than enough accumulated power from the family to rein you in if necessary."

Jess smiled brightly, and the other deceased family members raised their teacups.

Their party included ice giants, two fey that had died during childbirth and a few mages in the direct family. The rest of the invited dead were family friends and ancient teachers.

Jess looked out over those assembled and Benny shining like a bright star in their midst. Three hundred years ago, Jess had known that she was destined to be the companion of a melded being, she just didn't know how.

Her death at the hands of a lightning strike had escaped her precognition, but it had given her the charge to retain consciousness in the afterlife. The arrangements had already been made, and her transfer into a spectral being had been surprisingly natural. After that, she just had to wait until Benny entered the world.

In the strictest of senses, Benny was a relation. Across four generations and several removals, Benny was her cousin.

"Do you have any more directions for Benny?" Lettice smiled.

Jess looked over the party and saw the three men causally arranging themselves in a protective detail that was only visible to the trained eye. Benny didn't have anything to worry about, and soon, she would be authorised to use all that she knew to defend those around her.

Jessamine Turing raised her teacup. "Nope. She is doing just fine on her own."

Author's Note

Well, this isn't really a start. The first book in this universe was *Under his Claw*. Dragons and sex and all kinds of shenanigans. Zora and Regick were the players.

Book one felt good to write and 60 days from the release of *One Part Human, Two Parts Demon* will be out in which we face Benny's basic training and the side effects of her rather public exposure, as well as the actions of her parents thirty years earlier.

An Obscure Magic is a new universe with new characters, and at this point, I have over thirteen titles planned, rang-ing from valkryies, the inheritance of a magical practice ground, and how Freddy gains autonomy from the demon zone, plus much, much more.

I hope I am off to a good start in my little self-published universe.

Thanks for reading,

Viola Grace

http://www.violagrace.com
viola@violagrace.com

About the Author

Viola Grace (aka Zenina Masters) is a Canadian sci-fi/paranormal romance writer with ambitions to keep writing for the rest of her life. She specializes in short stories because the thrill of discovery, of all those firsts, is what keeps her writing.

An artist who enjoys a story that catches you up, whirls you around and sets you down with a smile on your face is all she endeavours to be. She prefers to leave the drama to those who are better suited to it, she always goes for the cheap laugh.